The Crocodile Prize Anthology 2011

The Crocodile Prize Anthology 2011

ISBN: 978-0-9871321-0-9

Cover: A Gogodala shield with crocodile motif from the Aramia River in Western Province carved by Namulu Mamena, originally from Kini village but now living in his wife's village of Aketa. The cover for this first Crocodile Prize anthology is modelled on the cover of Vincent Eri's ground breaking novel.

Sir Vincent Serei Eri (1936-1993)

The Crocodile, by Vincent Eri, was the first novel to be written by a Papua New Guinean, and was published by Jacaranda Press in 1970.

Vincent Eri was born in Moveave in Gulf Province and later became Director of Education, Papua New Guinea's first Consul General in Australia, a Member of Parliament and Governor General.

His novel is set in Papua New Guinea before and during World War II and is a coming of age story about Hoiri, whose life poses a continuing contradiction between traditional life and the modern world.

CONTENTS

OUR SPONSORS

We would like to thank you all for your generous contributions and hope you will stay with us in the years to come.

AustAsia Pacific Health Services

Barbara Short

Bob Cleland

Firewall Logistics

Interoil

Jackson Wells

Niuminco

Oilmin Field Services

Ok Tedi Mining

Pacific Bookhouse

PNG Attitude

PNG Post Courier

Robin Lillicrapp

Sasol New Guinea

South Pacific Social Solutions

SP Brewery

FORWARD

The Crocodile Competition evolved out of Keith Jackson's *PNG Attitude* website in a somewhat serendipitous manner.

As the readership of the website has grown the number of contributors has also expanded. In 2010 Patrick Levo, the features editor at the *PNG Post Courier* and a reader of the website, invited a number of contributors, myself included, to submit articles for the newspaper's annual Independence Day supplement.

Casting about for a suitable topic, I decided to write something about Papua New Guinean literature. I had been in Port Moresby in the years just prior to independence and knew that there had then been an enjoyable and vibrant literary scene. The University of Papua New Guinea was the important hub in those days.

I naively assumed that this had continued on into the post-independence period. I hadn't seen much evidence but guessed that as a local industry it might have a degree of invisibility outside the country. There was certainly a very active literary endeavour going on among expatriates like myself back in Australia. What I discovered was an unpleasant surprise; literature in Papua New Guinea was effectively dead in the water.

With a couple of notable exceptions in the work of people like Russell Soaba there was nothing in Papua New Guinea being published and, worse still, nowhere in the country to publish.

I mentioned this to Keith Jackson and jokingly suggested that he sponsor a literary completion. Keith took up the idea and Patrick Levo jumped on board to lend a hand.

We didn't know what would happen when we announced the competition. A previous attempt at getting Papua New Guinean contributors to dob in a corrupt politician had fallen flat and we half expected the same peculiar Papua New Guinean reticence to prevail over the competition. We were pleasantly surprised.

It is necessary to record that, while we have had a great response to the competition, all of the entries come from people who have access to a computer and the internet. This is understandable since it was launched from a website. What are missing are contributions from the people out in the villages who do not enjoy these amenities.

This is the one of the main reasons for publishing the anthology. By distributing it as widely as possible we hope to encourage those writers hiding out in the bush. This is why we have produced it as cheaply as possible. We want to uncover the literary talents of all of Papua New Guinea and we hope the anthology will do that.

We have assessed the entries included in the anthology on their originality and relevance to Papua New Guinea, along with their "grabbing" power. We were especially interested in pieces with a distinct flavour and style. We think there is a distinct Papua New Guinean school of writing out there, just as there are distinct Papua New Guinean styles of art. This is what we want to encourage.

For these reasons we have not placed too much emphasis on technical aspects or modern literary conventions; we don't think these are especially relevant.

In presenting the anthology we have also forsaken any attempt at cataloguing the entries by theme or subject.

One of the reasons for doing this is that it is too hard and we don't feel confident enough to do it. Instead we've opted to present the entries in alphabetical order of author in each category – short stories, poems, essays. We hope you don't find it too confusing. We also hope you enjoy the entries as much as we have.

Reading all the entries has been a very pleasurable and enlightening experience. To an outsider like me the short stories, poems and essays of Papua New Guinea say much about its society.

The policy makers in Papua New Guinea would do well to read the works in this anthology.

Repression of the press and the media is a primary tactic of control in repressive and dictatorial regimes. The press in Papua New Guinea is refreshingly free because of guarantees in the Constitution. This freedom has never been successfully challenged. It is interesting to speculate why there has never been a government-sponsored writer's support and publishing scheme however.

There is no doubt that a healthy community of writers and thinkers has tremendous influence.

Writers can help change the way society thinks and works.

To quote one of our writers in the competition: *I believe that the best we can do, as writers, is reveal what we are thinking and feeling, as different people from all walks of life."*

"Understanding each other better is a crucial step in learning to live together, preparing to realise the aspirations of our sovereign state, and to define our nationhood.

In this vein I would say to the writers, poets and essayists of Papua New Guinea that you are probably the most important people in the country. Whatever you do and whatever happens in the future you must keep writing. The future of your country may depend upon it.

Philip Fitzpatrick
September 2011

THE 2011 CROCODILE PRIZE WINNERS

2011 was the inaugural year for Papua New Guinea's national literary prize. There were four categories, short stories, poetry, essays and women's literature.

On the far left is **Martyn Namorong**. He won the 2011 Sean Dorney award for his essay *The Political Economy of Everything That's Wrong in Developing PNG.*

Alongside Martyn is **Lapieh Landu**, who won the Dame Carol Kidu prize for women's literature, which included her poems *His New Way* and *The Fighter,* and her essay *Island Home Conversion.*

Next to Lapieh is **Jimmy Drekore**, winner of the John Kasaipwalove poetry prize for his poem *Walking Barefoot to be Educated.*

And on the far right is **Jeffrey Febi**, who won the Russell Soaba short story prize for his story *A Song for Camels.*

SHORT STORIES

Seduction at the Hotel Cecil
By Kela Kapkora Sil Bolkin

It was a Friday the 20th of July 1969.

Yalgol was hard at work slicing, cutting and cooking in the kitchen of the Pacific Islands Regiment at Igam Barracks in Lae. He had landed the job after his experience as a cook, driver and catechist with the Catholic Church missionaries up in the Galkope territory in the Simbu Province.

His supervisor was Captain Fiona Ryles, who was the Royal Quarter Master (RQM). She was 23 years old and in charge of the food rations distributed to the Officers' mess, Senior NCO's and ORS messes and its stock upkeep.

Yalgol cooked and served in the Officers mess. Captain Ryles normally came in to eat at the mess after delegating jobs to the cooks. He had served her on several occasions when she came to dine. He was much taller and more muscular than his Highlands countrymen who had joined the military. He looked more like a well-trained soldier than most of the real soldiers at the barracks.

Captain Ryles admired Yalgol's tall frame and rippling muscles as he innocently went about doing his job. Yalgol tended to be intimidated by white women and didn't notice that she lusted after him.

One Friday afternoon as Yalgol was chopping up a large slab of beef the captain entered the kitchen. Yalgol was alone.

"Yalgol! You are working very hard."

"Yes, Captain! What can I do for you?"

"Will you escort me to town this evening?"

"Yes, Captain, I will," he replied without thinking.

"I'll pick you up at the junction of the Laborers' Compound and the Barracks Headquarters at 5:30 pm. Get yourself dressed up and wait for me there."

"Yes, Captain."

Captain Ryles lived in the European Married Quarters. She entered her apartment at 5:00 pm and unbuttoned her military uniform and dropped it into a bucket. Then she walked into the shower with her towel. She glanced quickly at her naked body in the mirror and smiled. Then she turned on the taps and ducked under the water.

Water drizzled on her smooth Queensland skin. Her mind was fixed on the young cook at the labourer's quarters. "I will teach that young Highland Hercules to make love tonight," the Toowoomba bred beauty whispered to herself. She was lost in the world of day dreams but finally came back to reality. She turned off the water and grabbed her towel from its hook and gently dried her wet shining body.

She walked to her wardrobe and dropped the towel wrapped around her breasts to the floor. She gently rubbed her skin with the Pacifica Body Oil bought in Brisbane during her last leave. While softly humming a melody she pulled on lacy pink underwear and a matching bra. The underwear and the bra were French made. She adjusted the bra over her large breasts so that it was nicely firm. Then she took a baby doll dress from her wardrobe and pulled it down over her head to cover her perfectly feminine body.

She brushed her hair with military precision and made her lips cherry red with lipstick. Last but not the least she pulled on black knee high boots, which transformed her into a sexy cowgirl from far North Queensland. Finally, she flexed to and fro in front of the mirror and fluttered her eyes and smiled.

"Huah!" she grunted. She looked absolutely gorgeous.

At the same time, at the fringe of the Labourers' Compound, Yalgol had a good bath with Klina soap under the shadows in a banana patch. He made sure nobody looked through the worn out bag walls that fenced the shower area.

He dried himself with a small hand towel and hurried back to the shed where he slept. He checked through the few clothes crumpled in a corner of the room where he slept and pulled on a pair of long grey trousers and tightened them with a worn old leather belt. His heart beat was rising with the thought of going out with a white woman.

"I have to polish my boots," he said to himself. There were kids playing in the nearby field and their noise drowned out the sound of any approaching cars. I'd better hurry in case I miss the car he thought.

He poured some coconut oil onto his pair of army issue boots and polished them before sinking his big feet into them. At the door way he picked up a broken mirror and struggled to see his face. He realized that he hadn't combed his hair and did so immediately. Then he strolled out of the battered old shed.

He had finished getting ready sooner than he thought and he hummed a courtship song as he strolled down to the junction at the Barracks headquarters to wait for Fiona to arrive.

Fiona hung a crocodile skin bag on her right shoulder and left her apartment and jumped into her jeep. She turned on the ignition. She drove past the Barracks and Officers' Mess and turned left. The Jeep came to a halt where Yalgol stood. He automatically started to jump in the back of the jeep but the Captain said, "Come and sit with me in the front." Yalgol withdrew his right leg from the rear and moved into the seat next to the Captain. Yalgol smelt the aroma of the captain and very much liked it but he didn't have the nerve to tell her that she smelled and looked lovely.

Fiona shifted the gears and the jeep was on the road again. They sped over the Bumbie Creek Bridge and reached the gate. The jeep came to a halt with the engine running. The guard seeing Captain Ryles in the car pushed a lever and the gate lifted into the air.

"Pass through!" he shouted and saluted.

"Thank you!" said Captain Ryles.

The soldier nodded his head as if saying, you're welcome.

The jeep roared forward into what is now Independence Drive in the dusk with the head lights on. They drove through East Taraka and the newly established University of Technology. They reached Omili without much conversation and continued onto the Butibum Road and reached China Town. When they were about a kilometre from the Hotel Cecil Fiona slowed down and they quietly turned onto the Voco Point Road and halted in front of the famous hotel.

The Hotel Cecil had been built in the mid-1930s to accommodate the growing European population after gold had been found at Eddie Creek near Wau in 1926. In those days the social life of the whites revolved around the hotel, which the New Guineans were strictly forbidden to enter.

"Darling, I want you and me to drink and be merry tonight. But rule number one. You must be by my side every single minute," said the Captain.

"Yes, Captain. I …. will take care of you," said Yalgol.

"Good, Darling," said the captain and extended her hand to Yalgol.

Yalgol timidly shook her hand but the Captain gave it a firm shake.

They entered the Hotel Cecil. The interior terrified Yalgol and he shivered. He had never been to such a place before. Four fifths of the people in the bar were Europeans. He timidly followed Fiona to a small round table. They pulled out two stools and sat facing each other.

Racial segregation was still strong in the army where Yalgol was employed despite the amendments to the ordinances after the war. In the army and the goldfields at Eddie Creek Europeans still used names like bush kanaka and boi to refer to Papuan New Guinean men.

Yalgol was very conscious of the *keep your distance look* he got from European officers and business executives with Fiona so close to him. She quickly realized that he was not at ease in the hotel.

"Darling, you and I are from the military. The ones you see in here are from the business community in Lae. They must fear us. Don't worry about anybody in here. You and I must enjoy our drinks and the night," she said.

Her sermon bolstered Yalgol's confidence and he re-gathered the toughness learned during his initiation in the men's hut years ago. "Just wait! I'll drink two or three stubbies and I should be okay," he replied.

"Madam, are you all right?" asked the bar girl who hailed from Salamaua. She had tattoos all over her exposed skin but Yalgol quickly looked away knowing very well that the Captain had her eyes on him.

"Two glasses of gin with tonic and orange juice," ordered the Captain. She pulled some bills out of her hand bag and smiled at Yalgol.

The bar girl returned with the two glasses and placed the tray on the table in front of the Highlander Hercules and the sun baked Queensland beauty.

"Thank you." The Captain looked at Yalgol and smiled. Yalgol took one of the glasses and the captain the other.

"Cheers!" said the Captain and Yalgol lifted his glass and said the same thing.

They sipped their drinks and looked around the room. It was noisy and Yalgol compared it to the noise of a funeral in his Galkope homeland. The lights were not very bright. The Beatles song *"Lucy in the sky with diamonds"* played in the room and was occasionally drowned out by intermittent laughter and loud voices. Fiona was on a mission; to have the Galkope lad succumb to her seduction.

As the minutes and hours ticked into the night Fiona kept buying drinks and gin and tonic flooded their table. They drank and talked as if they were an old couple. Slowly the alcohol took control. Fiona on several occasions lifted her right leg under the table and pressed hard into Yalgol's groin. Every time she pressed she smiled and held Yalgol's hands hard and squeezed. Yalgol felt his serpent awake and start to look for prey.

The Galkope man was not in his teens. He could read the signs perfectly well. He knew what that foot in his groin meant. His adrenaline rose and his heart beat accelerated.

"I will give you what you want. I have brought home many women. I am not a small boy," he whispered in his own Bari language.

Simultaneously, Fiona softly said, "I will take you to my apartment and you will undress me, Highlander Hercules?"

"Who am I to say no to such a beautiful woman? I will take you into your bedroom," said Yalgol for the first time with assertiveness. Fiona lifted her right hand and took Yalgol's left hand and gently stroked each finger.

It was already 12:30 am. The Captain belched and then said, "My Darling, we will leave for my apartment. It is now your turn to drive us home."

"Captain, it is not a problem. Trust me. I will take you safely home," said the Galkope man and extended his hand. The Captain clung on his tree trunk right hand and he cradled her to the jeep.

Yalgol rummaged around in her bag for the jeep's key and found it. He held her in his left hand and opened the door with his right hand. Then lifted her and sat her on the front seat and closed the door. He walked around to the other door and pushed it open and sat before the steering wheel.

"I want you in me," said Fiona and leaned toward Yalgol. She pushed her left hand into his muscular chest. "Kiss me, man!" she whispered. The full moon was just above the bay of Salamaua. Yalgol had a kind of reverence for nature, including the moon. The bright light made him uneasy.

"Not here. It's too public. I think; I'd prefer taking you to a place where nobody watches what we do," he replied and cranked the engine of the jeep.

"They can mind their own bloody business," shouted Fiona.

"The night is still young, Captain. Patience is a virtue," intoned Yalgol and steered onto the gravel road.

The vigilant guard saw the jeep come to a halt at the Igam Barracks gate. It was a typical army jeep. He didn't care who was driving it. He drowsily shouted, "Pass through."

Yalgol had his foot on the accelerator as soon as the gate ascended. The jeep came to a standstill in front of Fiona's residence. Yalgol quickly opened the door and got out. He opened the door to her house and came back for her. He opened the jeep's door for her but she wanted him to lift her and carry her. He lifted her off the seat and carried her in his big arms. He felt her breasts against his shoulder and his trousers were tight with his stiffness.

He sat her on the couch and returned to lock the door. After looking the door he returned but stopped short. He could not believe what he saw. The baby doll dress was on the floor. Captain Fiona Ryles was naked and looking straight at him. Their eyes met and she smiled.

"Walk straight to me, buddy," she said. She signalled with the index finger of her right hand.

Yalgol was shell shocked. He walked to where she stood like a naughty school boy before his head teacher. All this time he had only been able to imagine what was inside the military uniforms she wore. Now he could see what it had covered. He loved it.

Warmil's Spirit Bride
By Kela Kapkora Sil Bolkin

A kind hearted Bari youth named Warmil, who had lost his father during the warfare with the Gena people, settled with his mother and three small brothers at Morua Kaupa Nil Awil. His mother was called Kokil Gup Ku. His three brothers were Kipir, Kulkan and Arkal Ku.

Warmil grew up and soon filled the vacuum left by his father. He was strong and had already matured by his teens. At sixteen he built a hut and made a couple of gardens with the help of his three brothers for their mother. Kokil Gup Ku was very fond of them all. One dawn the sun emerged in splendour to the east. Mt. Elimbari and the red burning ball of the sun rubbed shoulders. The horizon to the east sent out yellow reddish rays to the Galkope land.

The early red burning ball of the sun on the horizon foretold yet another hot day even though a long streak of white cloud covered Porol, Woti, Bakl, Willa and Dinima. Young Warmil took his hunting weapons and strolled down to the river junction. Half way down he felt trickles of sweat on his forehead.

"It is very hot and humid. Where shall I go?" He had yet to decide between Kel Au Suna, Kel Gar and Sin Kaula. I must keep a vigil in the hut beside the river junction at Kel Au Suna. It's quite hot and the birds will frequent the hollow tree trunk for water. The last time I killed birds there they equalled all the fingers on both my hands. I'll try and go beyond that now and include my toes, thought Warmil.

The junction sieved the Wara Simbu, which snaked its way down from the north and the Wahgi River, which pushed its way east. At the Y-junction he saw the two different coloured rivers blend with ease as in unison they squeezed through the basalt rocks to the south east.

He stood at the banks of the Wahgi River and stared at the strength of the current. Logs and other rubbish the river carried were whisked away by the currents. Above him birds flew from his side of the river to the other with ease. He admired the sight and wished he could fly like the birds and go to other places with such ease.

He halted his day dreaming and brushed through the low bushes. He bulldozed past the shrubs and passed a couple of tall trees. Before he reached his hut with its nearby hollowed tree trunk filled with water he came upon an ul tree. At the base of the tree were mountains of fruit scraps discarded by possums. He studied the place in detail and decided that he would come in the night to hunt the possums.

Later he reached the hut and hollow tree trunk. All the dew in the leaves had evaporated and the thirsty birds had converged on the water in the hollowed trunk. The vigilant Warmil killed a few large birds at midday when the sun was strong. He took them home in the afternoon to roast for dinner.

At dusk the weather was fine, but windy and chilly. The vivid moon popped its head over the horizon where Mt. Elimbari and the sky met. It was as if the moon had followed the exact route the sun had taken in the morning.

Warmil finished chomping on his taro and a big roasted bird. He then took his bows and arrows down from the logs stored above the fire place. "This is a good full moon. I will go and check the ul tree for possums to hunt," he chanted.

He strolled down to Kel Au Suna. At Kel Au Suna people who fall in the Wahgi River upstream and drown while trying to cross eventually float down to the river pool there. People who lose relatives to the river normally walk down to Kel Au Suna to retrieve their bodies. He could see images of dead men facing up and women facing down floating at Kel Au Suna clearly in his mind.

Fear gripped him and he flinched at every sound produced by the creatures of the land as well as the rustling sound of the river. He cursed and knocked his head with his right hand. The scary pictures in his head vanished. He took a deep breath and walked with care as he followed the Wahgi River up towards the ul tree.

Out of the blue he saw a figure in the evening light picking the fruits of the ul tree and he felt his adrenalin set in motion. He rubbed his eyes with his right hand. The figure didn't look like a possum or that of any other animal. He swayed his head left and then right to make sense of what he saw.

When he got his bearing right he didn't believe what he saw. It was a young girl with a fur roped skirt and a band on each on her biceps. She also wore a necklace made of possum testes and had a light coloured bilum over her frizzy hair. The rays of the moon were reflected on her oiled breasts and goblet navel.

"Yal Kane!" winked Warmil to himself. He shivered and his pores bulged with goose bumps. At the same time he perspired in the full moon as if the sun was right above. "She is only human. I can jump forward, grab and tame her. I am a man, should she struggle to free herself I can wrestle her to the ground and hold her firmly until she gives in," he assured himself under his breath.

While the girl was still busy picking the fruits, Warmil left his weapons and crawled forward. When he was close enough he leapt forward and grabbed her. He firmly wrapped his hands around the trunk of her bare upper body just as she flinched. He clamped her in a vise-like grip.

She struggled but to no avail. Then she changed herself into all the many animals found in the area, including snakes and lizards. In this way she thought Warmil would be afraid and let her go. However Warmil held on to whatever being she changed into with conviction. In the end she succumbed to his grip and returned to her previous being, a beautiful young girl.

Warmil held her for a couple of minutes to make sure she didn't change her being again. He smelt the natural aroma of the wilderness in the girl. That fragrance was what Adam smelt when he first met Eve in the Garden of Eden.

The struggle came to an end and Warmil eased his grip and pulled his hands off with utmost reverence for the young girl. She took some time to regain her composure and then looked at Warmil with eyes sparkling like the moon above.

"I am a gil ap who used to live in the wilderness and fed on fruits. Your night is my day; hence, I came to harvest. If you were a lesser man you would have panicked and let me go. But you were truly courageous. For this reason, I am at your mercy."

Warmil's heart beat doubled. He had never seen such a beautiful girl before. "You are the most beautiful girl I have ever seen in my life. Who am I to let you go? I will make you my bride."

As they stood and looked into each other's eyes the full moon just above them was bulging with envy. It shone with such splendour that a rat running into the dry leaves below and an owl sitting on the branches of the huge trees above could be easily seen.

Warmil lead the gil ap to his home with joy and pride. His mother and his three brothers were already fast asleep. He removed the logs piled across the doorway and they entered the family hut.

At dawn his mother took the gil ap to Morua Kaupa Nil Awil. The Bari men in the men's hut exited and shouted euphorically when they saw the girl. She was then officially made a woman and wife of Warmil. A feast was made at Morua Kaupa Nil Awil that afternoon. Kokil Gup Ku and the men at Morua Kaupa Nil Awil didn't know that she was a gil ap.

Warmil and the gil ap lived with joy as a couple. Never once did Warmil beat her, as was the custom of his clansmen with their wives. In the years that followed she had these children; Mor, Alauro, Bale, Dama Kuri and Daral.

In later decades animosity brewed as Warmil added a couple of women to his household as second and third wives. In one such quarrel she made known to her children that part of her being was from another cosmos. To this day the gil ap's descendants and their legacy are called the Warmil Gauma. They make up the bulk of the Bari 2 sub-tribe in the Simbu Province in this age and time.

A Song for Camels
By Jeffrey Febi

There was an abrupt scream. And Mihi stopped in his track. He turned slowly with his heavy load and there was no one in sight.

His heart jumped! And beat faster. Then his body started shaking in panic. The sudden rush of blood forced out sweat and compelled him to do something.

He quickly but carefully lowered his sun-dried coffee beans in the tightly packed, used white 20kg flour bag on the ground and ran downhill calling loudly.

"Somolieeeeee! Somolieeeee!" He didn't hear his quivering voice echoe across the jungle yonder.

Somolie, a short and thin but tough guy with really strong arms hanging from broad shoulders that defined his physique, could easily be hidden from his view by tall grasses; but he was not certain.

He stopped at a spot where some Kunai grasses have been bent under the weight of something. He stepped forward, carefully, and called out.

A desperate voice responded and he moved closer to the edge of a cliff. Then peered over and saw Somolie hanging desperately onto some vines and small branches.

Mihi breathed a deep sigh. And for the first time ever saw Somolie's bald head. It was smooth and shiny, even under the cliff's shadow. Mihi called down and asked if Somolie was alright. The response was positive.

Somolie's cap was missing and he dreaded the thought of losing it. He looked down and spotted his coffee bag. Fortunately, it had landed on a cluster of wild tiny species of bamboo that were growing there. And realised it was safer where it had landed than he was.

Somolie carefully climbed down, then retrieved his coffee bag. He managed to drag his bag back up to where a vine which Mihi threw down had landed.

When Somolie and his coffee bag were safely up on the track, they sat down to rest.

It wasn't the first time for such to have occurred. Many others have lost stuff including store goods such as cartons of SP Brown beer to the fast flowing river below. Men, women and children had all had their share of experiences on this steep stretch of Kuipi track; a shortcut over the Kuipi Mountain which constituted one half of a rather unforgiving gorge.

It is a major track and its users call it their highway. Upon it tonnes of garden food, coffee beans, store goods, building materials, and even coffins with corpses have been transported for years - after their only road became impassable to vehicles due to continuing neglect.

Mihi broke the silence. "You're lucky!" And pointed to a spot further down and remarked. "If it had been there; it's a plummet to certain death".

Somolie agreed with a weary nod as a vivid recollection of a recent fatal fall he had witnessed flashed across his mind.

Then he slowly stood up and caressed his bottom. "It hurts", he groaned. "Something has scratched my bottom", he continued, then jokingly checked his private parts to ensure their wellbeing. "All intact!" he declared with a grin, and ensured his cap sat well on his head.

Mihi let out a stifled laugh. He didn't want to offend Somolie, but he really wanted to laugh. The sight of Somolie hanging like a bald cuscus was funny. He bowed his head to conceal his beaming face.

Then Somolie started laughing. Mihi burst into laughter and they laughed together. Somolie managed to explain between laughs that he stepped aside to urinate and lost his balance. Then he threw his coffee bag and jumped after it.

After a good long laugh, Somolie shouldered his bag and followed Mihi up the track. They had to reach the top, which seemed further still, before the sun gathered all its strength.

As he was slowly climbing, Somolie began to sing a song; with a voice that seemed devoid of shock.

They call us camels. They call us white horses.
They call us semi-trailers. They call us many names.
Names of things we don't know much of.
We're they who walk with the strength of our fathers.
Those bygone men who had tamed angry rivers,
Appeased bellowing clouds and walked with mists.

Our coffee beans shall not go to waste!
Our coffee beans shall not go to waste!
O no - no - no; shall not go to waste!

Mihi joined and they sang with a certain pride that sent the song speeding downhill on the wings of a determined breeze.

Far below, an army of white bags in a long and winding line resembling a herd of camels on a journey came into view. When the song reached them, hearts were touched and moved. Many repeated the chorus and the gorge reverberated with their inspiration.

It is their song and they loved it. It inspires strength which they need in order to climb Kuipi; and confidence to walk shamelessly with their loads through villages (whose inhabitants ridicule and call them names) along the road.

And they continued singing their hearts out - husbands, wives and their children.

The Death of a Warrior
By Jeffrey Febi

Alone, Ooamie struggled against death's cold embrace until he died a terrible death in his bed.

A strange spell immobilized Ooamie's body and only his heart and lungs fought while everything froze. Doses of pain and suffering were slowly administered until he succumbed. What remained of him was a body stiff as dry wood with a cold stare; and the tip of his tongue vaguely visible from behind the back of a half opened mouth.

It was only three days ago when Ooamie suddenly fell ill. His unusual symptoms could not be connected to any type of sorcery, so he was taken to his haus-pik just outside the village. Hidden from prying eyes and ears, he would to be monitored closely by his wife Onekayai with assistance from Fetapa the orphan.

The haus-pik was typical; round with a low roof and a door barely a meter tall. It was big enough though, and could accommodate both his family and the pigs.

His brothers began seeking people who might have a cure. A couple of days had passed and Ooamie's condition worsened, observed Onekayai; but she could do nothing, so she did her best to nurse her husband. Fetapa couldn't care less, and went about doing his daily chores.

Often Fetapa, a pre-teenager, wonders where his parents are, and why they have deserted him. He didn't know his parents had both died: his mother while giving birth to him and his father from acute dysentery a few months later. No one had talked to him about his parents and he misses them.

Onekayai returned from a garden nearby. Over a huge kaukau bilum on her back, rested a bunch of bananas; and slung around her neck, a brown laplap held her sleeping child. As she jumped over the fence, she saw Fetapa with his small bow and arrows chasing lizards. He didn't see her until she spoke from behind. Fetapa froze then quickly turned and retort; "He's sleeping!"

Inside the haus-pik, Onekayai saw her husband's motionless figure on the bed. It's been like this for the last two days. She removed her load and breathed deeply; then carefully hung her child's laplap near her husband and instructed Fetapa to fetch water. She rested a little, and then drank from a bamboo Fetapa brought, and started the fire to bake kaukau for the evening.

Meanwhile, Ooamie's brothers returned from their journeys. In the haus-man they reported their findings. When finished, a long silence ensued; broken only by an occasional distant bark from a dog. All eyes were set on the fire as its flaming tails danced mockingly. Smoke reluctantly rose from tobacco pipes and no one was heard breathing in the frozen silence that engulfed them. Even the chief's two dogs lay silent under their master's bed.

The chief pondered intensely over the inevitable: who is responsible; how many will he order to be killed; who should execute his orders? Everyone realized their chief's deep concentration and no one dared interrupt him.

Then the dogs barked all at once. Startled, the chief dropped his pipe and burnt himself. Furious, he jumped off his bed, grabbed a piece of wood and started hitting at the dogs haphazardly. Those quick enough, got out of the way; others were unlucky. Someone was hit by a wood that slipped out of the chief's hand and he crashed into another person nearby. Then much confusion erupted and the flames died out but for a weak flicker.

Standing outside, Fetapa heard much noise and commotion; but no light seeped through the gaps in the door. He heard dogs growling in pain as men shouting profanities beat them.

He cleared a lump in his throat and softly called out a name he was instructed to report to. "Ba-ua-ti!" No response came. He called louder; "Bauati!" No response again. There was still much noise when a voice called for calm and someone to attend to the fire. He called again at the top of his voice; "Bauati!" Then voices ordered each other to stop talking, and there was silence.

Fetapa trembled, but he mustered some courage to call again. After what seemed like eternity, a deep and hoarse voice demanded; "Who's there?" He responded quickly and the door opened. He felt warm air brush against his face; it felt good. Then he peered into the dimly lit house and saw figures with unblinking stares. The chief, Bauati, knew what Fetapa's unexpected appearance meant. Then Fetapa broke the news, but anger deafened them, even Bauati wasn't listening.

When tears started to flow, a tirade of obscenities from Bauati quickly forced them dry. Then with a calm but stern voice he gave out precise instructions, and everyone knew exactly what to do. It was a simple plan; a plan to avenge Ooamie's death. It must be done or their inaction would bring shame to their clan.

Bauati quickly dispatched some men to secure and guard Ooamie's haus-pik, with instructions to talk to no one regarding the death. Fetapa scurried behind to catch up with the fast walking men. The risk of potential contamination from the killers who could sneak into the haus-pik using spells was great; and this would make it impossible to find out those responsible for Ooamie's death.

After much deliberation, four strong men stepped out of the haus-man; followed closely by Bauati, and two older men. Armed with bamboo torches, bows and arrows and knives, they hurried to the haus-pik. A few meters behind, three women trailed. Malufovi, Bauati's wife and two elderly women kept their distance from the men.

Bauati and his men entered the haus-pik and closed the door behind them. The women gathered around a fire under a temporary shelter Onekayai had erected. Fetapa was there too, but no one took notice of him. After a while the door squeaked open and figures stepped out and disappeared into the dark.

The women entered the haus-pik and eyed the corpse sorrowfully. They looked at the eyes; fierce warrior eyes once lit up with love and compassion for his family; they caressed the cold hands; strong hands that many times brought them food and meat. The legs felt soft and fragile; not the ones they've relied on for swiftness and power. They didn't see a warrior tonight, rather, a husband and son they would miss dearly.

Their hearts broke and they sobbed into the night. Their heads ached but still they sobbed. Ooamie's wife wanted to cry out loud but she couldn't. She wanted to sing to her husband's ghost in the rocks yonder; to tell him he will be missed; their child would be fatherless; and his kaukau was still by the fire place. She wept bitterly. The others were strong and wise women; the very reason they were asked to come. They ensured she did not make sobbing sounds. If she did, the guards around the fence didn't hear any. And this was to be the order of things; silently grieve until Ooamie's death was avenged. So far it was good.

They heard the first insect chirp as dawn approached. More insects joined and the early dawn reverberated with chaotic sounds. Their hearts heaved with anxiety as a bamboo-pot was pushed further into the heart of the fire and watched closely. Malufovi ensured the pot did not burn, but it steamed violently as droplets of liquid hissed into vapour.

Then they heard a faint sound; a pleasant tune amidst much noise. They listened hard and only heard; "two for Ooamie and one for Bauati!" It seemed distant still, but Malufovi removed the bamboo from the fire; emptied its contents on banana leaves and they gathered around to eat.

As he stepped over the fence, Bauati called out to his wife exhaustedly; "Women can cry aloud now! Women can cry aloud now!"

Fetapa was woken from his sleep by joyful singing and weeping. But he felt hungry and moved to the fireplace to search for leftovers. He felt a soft and round thing on a stone by the fireplace. It was fleshy so he sniffed it. It felt like meat and he tasted it. Then placed it in his mouth and bit into it. It was food alright, and he started chewing it.

Word reached other clan members in the village and soon they all gathered at the haus-pik. Many cried openly and sang old songs about warriors who flew with cockatoos on the yonder rocks.

Suddenly Malufovi realized she had left the testes on a rock by the fireplace. She rushed into the house and searched but to no avail. She went out and saw Fetapa chewing on something nearby. She enquired and Fetapa told her what he was chewing. Malufovi angrily ordered him to spit it out into her hands and he reluctantly obliged.

Two days of mourning had passed, and Bauati realized Ooamie's corpse was missing its sex organ. Further checks revealed a piece from the left inner thigh missing too. He knew the mothers loved and would miss Ooamie dearly. Then with a chuckle and a slight nod, he ordered the corpse be buried.

The Twin Treasure
By Bette Carinya Kare

Viper and Vixen are a distinct pair of twins that can never be distinguished, even by their own parents. Unless they turn to show the different coloured streaks of hairs above their right ears (which are natural), they can never be told one from another.

Both twins have the same ebony, nape-length hair, red-flushed skin, and cute button noses. Viper and Vixen are seven-year-olds who love history, archaeology and excavating ancient treasures, and both look nothing like their parents of Norwegian ancestry.

Some people think the twins were adopted, while a few suppose they are not Mr. Varte's children. The twins can never come out of their house because of a curse in the Varte lineage. The only times they are seen outside are at the local preschool and church.

Now Victor Varte is the only child in his family and coincidently Erin Varte is so, too. But one fine, sunny day, she had a knock on the door. As Erin Varte answered it, a middle-aged man vigorously wrapped her in his arms instantly. Erin Varte was surprised, but also confused. He let her free after a long tearful hug and says, "*I've been looking for you everywhere. I am Gaston, your half-brother.*" Mrs. Varte never knew about having a sibling but she was too ecstatic to be reasonable.

Gaston was invited for dinner the following weekend and was introduced to Victor Varte and the twins. After dinner Gaston began chatting with the twins and discovered they had the same interest in discovering old artefacts. Gaston had an excavation site and invited his niece and nephew to visit it one time. The twins had to get permission before they went anywhere. The parents allowed them but on a condition that they be back before noon.

Vixen and Viper were taken out of town to an isolated area. The site was actually a cave where they had to brush dirt away and dig up artefacts among the debris. This became a continuous habit each weekend; looking for clues to find rare materials.

One weekend, while the twins were away with their uncle Gaston, Erin asked Victor to explain the curse, and Victor replies, "A long time ago, the Great Varte used two precious stones to heal the sick and to bring prosperity to unfortunate people. But he destroyed the stones because he had an assistant who had an evil motive; he wanted the stones to gain power and wealth. In the future, they would reincarnate to destroy the evil assistant, who would live longer to try to possess them..." Erin interrupts frustrated, "You are not saying my kids are mere, rare rocks, are you?" Victor sadly responds, "Viper, our boy, is the Sapphire Serpent, and that is why he has blue streaks of hair, while our Vixen is the Ruby Fox. Both have reincarnated through the Varte bloodline to destroy the evil assistant once and for all."

Back at the site, Gaston and the twins discover an old and torn papyrus scroll amongst the debris. The scroll has hieroglyphics drawn on it. Gaston attempts to decipher the strange language. After a moment of hard thinking, he laughs mockingly. The children think they find a treasure. Gaston pulls out a golden dagger, and attempts to thrust it into the twins. Before he stabs them, Viper flicks out a forked tongue and bites him on the neck, and Vixen wags a fluffy tail and scratches his face. The Sapphire Serpent and the Ruby Vixen take form. Gaston shouts in pain as poison from the bite and scratches numb his body. He cries out for the pain was agonising. All the parts of his body start to dry up until he bursts into thin air. Gaston, the evil assistant, had been destroyed.

Mr. and Mrs. Varte arrived to see no sign of life or movement. In the dim light of their torch, they could see two precious stones gleaming on the floor of the cave.

The Blackbirders
By Carolus Ketsimur

There was hardly any cloud in the sky. From the vast blue above, the tropical morning sun shone brightly on Banio Bay, revealing a deep blue horseshoe-shaped expanse ringed by a narrow brown strip separating the sea from the green forest, which ran gently towards the mountain ranges in the distance.

Just beyond the southern corner of the bay, the kunai-covered Re'an Hills seemed out of place in the lush green Bougainville vegetation. The hills were the remains of a huge volcanic eruption of a long time ago – of which no-one knew.

It was low tide. Almost everybody was out on the reef. The men lined the edge of the water, casting strings attached to bamboo rods into the gently breaking waves. The women walked slowly along the dry reef, baskets in hand, collecting shells, crabs and anything else they came across. Black figures darted here and there, chasing the unfortunate fish caught in pools left behind by the receding water.

On the beach children played in the sand, as one or two dogs roamed the village looking for something to eat. White smoke rose lazily from the village to be dispersed by the breeze.

Then around the southern point, an object slowly turned into the bay. All movement stopped as eyes turned towards the object now travelling slowly along the coast. After a while people started moving again, coming together in groups to discuss what they saw. Was it some kind of a big canoe? What was that big post standing on top? Wouldn't the weight of that post cause a capsize? And what was that noise and smoke?

As the thing got closer, white figures could be seen moving around. It was obvious this was a ship of some sort, towing a much smaller vessel. When the cutter came level with the crowd, it stopped and the small dinghy was pulled from behind.

Three white men carrying sticks got into the dinghy and pushed off. As the dinghy nosed in to the reef, the crowd sensed something. A few people slowly moved away; others hovered uncertainly. Some wanted to turn and run, but their curiosity was too strong. They wanted to stay and see what these white men would do.

The white men jumped off the dinghy and ran towards the crowd. Some of the crowd broke and ran and one of the white men pointed his stick up to the sky. There was a sharp cracking sound and smoke appeared at the end of the stick. The running men stopped and hesitated. This was enough to let the white men catch up. They grabbed three men and proceeded to tie their hands with rope.

The rest of the villagers ran as the three captured men were half dragged to the dinghy and taken aboard the cutter.

While all this was going on, a lone fisherman moved around the reef towards the Tsunpets River mouth, showing no interest in the unfolding drama. He had stopped to look at the vessel as it rounded the point into the bay and then gone back to his business, as if nothing unusual was happening.

Having got the three captives aboard, the cutter moved off towards the river mouth. It stopped, and the dinghy pushed off with the three hunters aboard. As it came to the reef the white men jumped off and hurried, half running, towards the lone figure.

With the rest of the villagers gone, the hunters' intention was to grab anyone they could find. In that state of mind they did not realise how small was their present prey. Two men grabbed him, one on each arm, and propelled him, half carrying him, back to the dinghy then to the cutter.

He did not show much fight as they bundled him on to the ship, which started moving again past the mouth of the Tsunpets River. Further on, it stopped once more and two more captives were taken before the vessel moved on towards the entrance of the Bay.

It was just after midday as the cutter headed out of Banio Bay. Back on shore women and children wept and people wondered whether they would see their men again. They had no idea where the boat had taken them. On the ship the captives sat huddled inside the hold, eyes darting here and there as if looking for ways to escape.

The smallest one did not show much anxiety. He was calm and sat there quietly. None of them spoke. They did not know it, but they were on their way to the cane farms of Queensland. Whether they liked it or not did not really matter.

Country Road, Take Me Home
By Eva Kuson

"Country road, take me home to a place I belong, west coast Nyada…"

These are not the original words of John Denver's country hit, but a made up one by John Silas, an old singer in my village.

My village Nyada is located on the western coast of Manus Province. So it would be fitting to mention 'Nyada' to convey a bit of pride among eager young listeners who flocked the beach to listen to John Silas sing.

He was an old, lean man with bushy eyebrows and moustache. He always tied a grey dusty laplap around his waist, wore a red cap and carried his small handmade ukulele in his worn out basket wherever he went.

My granddad once told me that he made his name up because his real name meant excreta in the local language. I refused to accept that story because as far as I was concerned John Silas was a singing legend.

He had a fluent English accent, a gentle voice and loved singing old country songs from Slim Dusty, Lobo, Kenny Rogers and John Denver.

Every Sunday evening children and young men gathered around on the beachfront and listen to him sing his heart away. He would nod his head and shake his knees under his dusty laplap and sing with his eyes closed until the song ended.

He usually refused the offer of a guitar; he preferred his old rugged ukulele. He plucked, picked and strummed the ukulele like a pro singer in the old country movies we watched, which would be greeted with hearty laughter and applause from the audience.

At the end of his singing he would play some local songs and everyone joined him in different harmonies. Small boys would protest ari jah (one more) but he'd tell us to go home because our mothers might chase him and burn his ukulele.

Although he was a great singer he spent most of his time alone in his small kitchen on the beach crafting canoe paddles, wooden bowls and ukuleles.

One legend had it that, in his young days in Australia, he used to sing with Slim Dusty. And the other was that he was an Aborigine who ran away and settled in Nyada. There were many tales about this wonderful, gentle singer.

My grandma told me that they all grew up together and he later moved to Rabaul and worked on the plantations there.

After several years he returned home with a Tolai lady, but due to ill luck, his wife died during child birth and his son died a week later. Ever since then he lived alone and his only company was his ukulele.

He talked little and rarely participated in community meetings and social events. Old women would gossip amongst themselves, at the back of their husbands during village gatherings, that he would contribute better if he talked just like his singing.

I remembered him quite well because he referred to me as Nadu Misis, meaning 'small white girl', whenever he saw me around the village, as I'm light in skin colour, different from the other children.

Four years back I went for holiday in Nyada and met him. The singer had grown smaller and I noticed old age was catching up.

He glanced at me and said, "Oh the small white girl had returned". He was still wearing his cap which had gone pink in colour and his laplap was cleaner.

I was overwhelmed with sadness when I saw that he was not carrying his only company, the ukulele.

"So you think I would sing forever?" he laughed.

I tried not to answer the question because I already knew the answer. He was old now and could barely hold his ukulele, or project his voice as he used to, or shake his knees and nod his head.

In those years growing up in the village, I developed the taste for country and old time music because of John Silas's singing. We never owned radios or MP3 or CD players, and were kept in the dark about the latest music, but his magical singing exposed us to country music.

I still love old country songs and I'm not really into all the crazy hip hop music and rap and rock and roll of today.

He passed away a week ago and I was saddened by his death because he was truly a great singer. He will surely sing with Slim Dusty now in the pub up in the clouds where there is no beer.

The country road has now taken him home to a place where he truly belongs. Heaven.

The Sound of Silence
By Pochon S Lili

Martha walked lifelessly through the colourful throng of people at the famous Gerehu bus stop in Port Moresby. Despite the fast approaching night she was in no hurry to go home.

The air was scented with the familiar smell of exhaust fumes from the many PMV's and one could hear the yelling of the PMV "bus crews" as they tried desperately to haul in as many passengers as possible before the night overcame them.

Lurking behind the bus stop shelters were gangs of scruffy looking young men, eyes scanning the crowd intensely in search of a potential victim whose wallet or mobile phone would finance Friday's drinking spree.

Street vendors, despite the late hour, continued to market their wares aggressively, decreasing their prices every now and then in an attempt to sell off the day's stock.

The young girl of eighteen years continued to walk home slowly, the bitterness and pain she was so used to feeling was gone now, replaced by an emptiness that only reminded her of the suffering she had endured for so long.

Martha remembered that fateful day vividly, the day when the nightmare began.

She was in Grade 8, a beautiful girl tanned by the unforgiving sunshine so typical of Port Moresby. Martha had finished school and was upstairs rummaging for food in the kitchen.

"Martha," boomed a deep voice from the living room.

The girl yelped in shock but then sighed in relief when she realised that it was only her father.

"Yes Daddy?" Martha responded.

"Come here." her father replied in a slurred voice.

Martha then realised that her father had been drinking. She walked stiffly to him, her legs shaking slightly. The unmistakeable stench of stale beer terrified her and already tears were forming in her eyes.

The man stared long and hard at his little girl with bleary eyes and as Martha stared back into those wild eyes she knew that this was no longer the man she called her father, her heart sank and she sensed without a doubt that something terrible was about to happen.

All of a sudden she wished she wasn't alone with her father.

Suddenly her father picked her up roughly and carried her into the bathroom where he abused her repeatedly telling her that she had been a naughty girl and he was punishing her. Martha was too shocked and confused to even cry or protest. She was 14 years old.

Four years later the memories of the continual sexual abuse at the hands of her father no longer conjured up the usual feelings of hurt or betrayal. Martha simply did not feel anything anymore.

People typically think of hell as being a raging inferno with hot flames, run by demons with pitch forks, but there is a different kind of hell, one where you are slowly devoured by your own thoughts, it is this kind of hell that some say is the worst of all.

Martha had passed the bus stop and was nearing the house in which she had suffered so much.

She almost smiled when she recognised the unmistakable sound of wailing coming from her house. Finally she had gotten her revenge. Her father would pay dearly for what he did to her, and so would the rest of her family for not realizing that she was being abused.

She had toyed with the idea for so long, she had replayed the scene over and over in her mind and she had gained no satisfaction when she finally did it, only a sense of closure, a sense of finality.

The cries were louder now and people were flooding into her yard as news spread of the terrible thing that had just happened. A feeling of doom hung ominously over the house and those who entered the house were consumed by the horrific spectacle before them.

Martha walked slowly into the yard and up the stairs into the house. The small house was packed to capacity but she did not have difficulty making her way into the small room.

Martha stared dreamily at her own dead body still hanging from the ceiling fan, tongue hanging out, arms and legs already stiffening in the cold, unforgiving embrace of death. With her ghostly eyes she looked long and hard at her father crying softly in the corner and wondered what he was feeling.

But what did she know about feelings anymore? For she was no longer of this world, rather she was an imprint of her former self, a member of the spirit world, a lost soul destined to spend an eternity searching for the life she never had.

Expect the Unexpected
By Francis Nii

Anis and Maria were a happily married couple. They both had well-paid government jobs and they lived in a high covenant house in Boroko, the nation's capital. They had two children, a three year old boy and a one year old girl.

Anis loved Maria so much. He found her to be the kind of woman he desired for a wife – beautiful, modest, obedient, loving, caring and very faithful. Anis wholeheartedly trusted Maria's fidelity. He had always boasted to his friends at social gatherings that under no circumstances would Maria give her love away to anybody else.

Maria found Anis to be a loving and caring husband and father, however there was one thing that had been bothering her since they got married. Anis had a tendency of going out on pay week Fridays and returning the next morning dead drunk. His body and clothes would smell of alcohol and perfume.

Maria suspected that Anis was having affairs with other women but she didn't bother much at first. However, since HIV was becoming endemic Maria felt that her life was at risk. She started to raise her concerns. Every time she raised the matter Anis would have nice excuses to cool her down. In the bottom of her heart Maria felt that Anis was lying to her.

As time went by Maria was feeling increasingly restless. There was no peace in her. She resolved to launch a secret investigation targeting the hotels as the starting point. And, as suspected, she found out that Anis was frequenting one particular hotel in the city with female companions. A waitress at the hotel known to Maria told her everything about Anis' promiscuity.

There were several women that Anis was dating. The waitress personally knew some of them and they were floozies. Anis would make them drunk and sleep with them in the hotel. They would check out very early the next morning.

Maria didn't take any immediate action. She went about with her normal life for she had not personally seen Anis with any woman yet.

One pay week Friday, as usual, Anis did not return home. Maria waited until dusk and she rang her waitress friend. The waitress promptly reported that Anis was already into the thick of the evening with one of his floozies. The waitress described the woman as Betty, a young teller who worked in a bank at Waigani. Maria thanked her and switched off the phone.

Anis and Betty drank until they were drunk, all on Anis' account. Then they slept together in room 16.

Early in the morning as Anis and Betty were making their way out the door to the next room in front squeaked open. A couple came out. The woman gave Anis an inscrutable smile and walked away hand in hand with her partner.

Anis got the shock of his life. He felt that his heart was going to burst out of his mouth. It was very painful. He stood still embracing his chest. Betty was scared. She thought Anis was dying. She supported him back to the room and rested him on the bed. After some minutes Anis felt better.

"The woman is my very wife. She slept right in the next room with that stranger and I didn't know," Anis told Betty as they walked out. It dawned on Betty that that was why Anis almost suddenly died of heartbreak.

Anis later learnt that Maria had taken a taxi to the hotel in the night just in time to see him and Betty move into room 16. Maria had deliberately booked room 15, courted the stranger and slept with him. In the morning as soon as she heard them moving out she came out with her partner to meet them – a deliberate ploy to give Anis the shock of his life. Instead she nearly killed him. Anis nearly had a nervous breakdown when he thought about Maria opening her legs to the stranger.

Anis thought Maria had gone out but she was at home when he arrived. The rancorous feelings about Maria opening her legs to the stranger rekindled. "What are you doing here Mrs Sex Libertarian? I thought you had gone!" Anis shot at her.

"Not necessary Mr Libertine. Why don't we apologise, forgive each other and promise never to engage in promiscuity again?" Maria replied coolly.

"Simply pack up and leave with the girl and leave the boy with me."

"No, I take both or I won't leave if you hold one back."

"Take them and leave now as it suits you," Anis finally resolved.

So it ended; the happy marriage of Anis and Maria. Surprisingly the breakup was simple, non-violent and amazingly it took only a few minutes. There was no squabbling, nor bash ups or lengthy litigation which are the common scenes in the lead-up to any divorce in Papua New Guinean society.

Maria went her own way with the two children and Anis went his own way with a bitter scar that would never be easily undone.

The saga of Maria and Anis signals that the tenet of male superiority and dominance in sexual practises and family life in Papua New Guinea is gradually fading away in this contemporary world.

Technological advancement, increased and sophisticated socio-economic and political knowledge and ideologies have paved the way for greater gender equity.

The male folks ought to treat their female counterparts with respect, dignity and loyalty as equals. Then the female folks in return will respect and be loyal to their male partners. However, if a male thinks that he is superior and is at liberty to practice promiscuity and his partner will remain faithful he is making a grave mistake. He can expect the unexpected and the consequences can rankle forever.

A Night to Remember
By Martyn Namorong

The labour ward at Port Moresby General Hospital was busy as usual that night. Women arrived, women waited and women delivered. The pungent odour of amniotic fluid mixed with the cold air-conditioned air sending a chill through the infants born that night. There was the usual sound tract of mothers and babies crying. The white walls and floor tiles glowed in the brightly lit room.

The medical student dressed in a white coat with a stethoscope hanging from his neck, paused as he looked at the women sitting on a single bench in the cold labour ward. Many held their backs and abdomen, their faces expressing the distressful events that were occurring internally.

Each woman looked at him pleadingly, wanting to be admitted into the ward. "Ol mama, sampela, wara buruk o nogat?" he asked in Pidgin. They all shook their heads. He couldn't admit them. All the beds were occupied. Only women about to deliver or presenting with complications were given priority.

He turned and walked to bed thirty-six. The young mother there kept screaming, "dokta plis helpim mi! Ayo, baby bai kamaut nau! Helpim me..." He examined her and noted his findings on her chart. She was primi-gravid – a first time mum and the baby wasn't coming anytime soon. He reassured her and left the cubicle.

As he walked past bed thirty-five, the nurse called him in to examine the mother. The nurse looked distressed and informed him of the mother's condition. She was grand-multi-parous; she had five children and was in labour for the sixth. Her blood pressure had shot through the roof and her consciousness was altered. She seemed stable though according to his assessment but they both decided they should consult the Resident Medical Officer on duty.

As he was chatting with the nurse, another voice wailed from the other end of the ward. "Dokta! Plis helpim mi, het b'lo baby kamaut nau!" He rushed over to the other end and arrived just in time. He delivered the head, shoulders and the rest of this beautiful baby girl. He placed the crying neonate on her mum's abdomen, clipped the umbilical cord and cut it. "Welcome to the cruel world, baby" he smiled as he spoke to her. He wrapped her in some clean cloth and handed her to her mum.

A couple of minutes later the placenta was delivered.

He then took the baby to the examination room. It was warm compared to the rest of the labour ward. It did not have the typical odour of aromatic compounds that was prevalent outside. The baby weighed 2.9 Kg. He administered a shot of Hepatitis B vaccine followed by Vitamin K. "I told you it was a harsh world," he laughed as she shrieked in his arms.

He took her to her mum, who seemed remarkably well composed compared to the past half an hour. This was what impressed him about all the women who came to deliver. They would progress from the extreme of pain during labour to total calmness after delivery. If there ever was a symbol for the power of the human spirit, it was the face of a woman during and after labour.

He looked at the clock on the wall, it was 12 am. He decided it was time to go back and have some rest at the student dormitory. He recorded the details of the delivery in the register and collected all his gear. He packed his stethoscope, pregnancy wheel, tape measure, thermometer and blood pressure cuff into his bag.

He removed his white coat and washed his hands in the basin. As he began walking out the back door he could see mothers in agony, looking at him from the bench in front. There by the corridor to the back door lay women with their babies on the cold white floor, waiting to be discharged the next morning.

He smiled and said goodnight to the night duty nurses. It was to be his last night at the labour ward.

One Night in Mosbi
By Martyn Namorong

On the evening of Tuesday 10th May, I had an argument with my parents and decided to sneak out at night at around 9pm. I changed into long black jeans, put on a black singlet and wore a black pinstriped long sleeve shirt. I walked to the living room where I put on my boots and a dark blue cap.

I asked my small brother where the gate key was and he said it was with dad. Dad usually takes the key when there's been trouble at home so that no one leaves.

I wasn't planning on going anywhere in particular; I just wanted to leave home. I have had enough.

I decided to climb over the fence. The fence is typical of many fences that surround the homes of city residents. Mesh wire wall with barbed wire and coils of razor wire on top. It is meant to keep criminals out and residents safe in their prison.

Anyway, I was able to scale the fence but as I jumped down to the other side, the razor wire caught my right arm and it was butchered. I did not even feel a thing until I felt blood oozing and to my horror I could see tendons.

Hearing the noise at the fence, my dad came over to investigate. I just told him I had slashed my hand and would probably be needing surgery and I left for the emergency ward at Port Moresby General Hospital.

When I arrived, I wasn't sure where to find the ward due to renovations currently being undertaken at the former site of the emergency room. I walked through the corridors of the hospital and was fortunate to come across a medical student who took me over for treatment.

The student was horrified by the look of the wound. It looked very vicious. She couldn't believe my story and thought I was drunk. I offered to allow her to smell my breath but she wasn't keen on it. Instead, I removed the shirt and she placed gauze over the wound and wrapped it up.

I was taken directly to the mini-theatre, where an adult male from Ialibu was being stitched up by the Resident Medical Officer. I knew the Resident from my days at medical school. He reassured me that I would be next to be treated.

As I sat in the theatre, I could feel the effects of the blood loss. I decided to lie down in order to avoid fainting. I was not in any sort of pain.

As I lay down, the relatives of the guy being stitched up took a keen interest in me. I told them I was a street vendor but they didn't seem to believe that story. Then I told them about my blog and the patient said he had seen it. One of the ladies decided to come over and wash the blood off my hands even though I protested against it. It was a very nice gesture because she did it without hand gloves. It was rather poignant for me because the first patient I had inserted an intravenous canula into was HIV positive and I had also done that without hand gloves.

It was around 10 pm and I was soon joined by Sibona, a young male from Porebada. He had injured himself while playing volleyball. He seemed in great pain and was restless. I decided to chat with him and try to distract his focus from the injury. I asked him if he had taken any pain killers and he said he had taken aspirin. I explained to him that aspirin prevents blood from clotting and that probably was the reason he was still bleeding albeit not profusely. He had a small cut relative to my gaping wound but he seemed far more agonized than I was.

The boy from Porebada decided to go out to get fresh air, leaving me alone. As I sat singing to myself, my dad called. I was mad and didn't want to answer his call. I sent him a nasty message and told him not to contact me. Anyway, the poor guy had followed me to the hospital but I had no intention of seeing him.

It wasn't until around 2:30 am that the Emergency registrar came over to fix me up. He was accompanied by a security guard. He told me to remove the gauze. It was glued to the wound by blood clots. He suggested that I remove it under running water. As the water ran over the wound I felt sharp tormenting flashes of pain and moaned loudly.

Surprisingly, when I had completely removed the gauze, the pain disappeared. I smiled and remarked, "Sweat!" That made the registrar smile and I walked over to the operating table to have the wound stitched. He anaesthetized the wound and the surrounding region, cleaned it with iodine and cut out the disfigured flesh to create a clean wound which he began suturing.

After suturing he washed the area with iodine, placed pads over the wound and bandaged it.

It was painless and the whole procedure took about 30 minutes. I helped the registrar clean up afterwards and we went to the drug station where I received some medication. I thanked him and left the hospital.

As I walked through the hospital car park I saw dozens of people sleeping in the shadows. Outside, more people slept by the roadside. I am not referring to those who pitch tents opposite the hospital. The people I'm referring to are the homeless of Port Moresby. They sleep on the pavement because it radiates heat during the night and is thus a warm surface to sleep on. Even though I was aware of these homeless people, I never knew there were so many of them.

I sat at Three-Mile bus stop watching movies at the canteen with other homeless people, until dawn.

It Only Happens in Fiction?
By Patricia Paraide

It was lunch time. I was hungry. I walked home dreaming of a nice egg sandwich for lunch. Our house is a five-minute walk from the office. I found my twenty-five year old nephew and our domestic helper, standing at the bottom of the steps. They both looked disturbed. "What is wrong?" I demanded.

"We heard Uncle's favourite hymns on the radio in there. He is not home. His office car is not here. The door is still locked. We have just arrived. We both heard the music. The radio was turned off this morning. We know that there is no one is in there. We are spooked," my nephew explained.

I looked at them and laughed. Then joked "Devil get them!" and walked up the steps. I unlocked the door with my set of keys and walked into the house. My nephew followed cautiously. I checked the computer, radio and stereo set. They were definitely switched off. I checked the bedroom. I checked the bathroom. My husband was definitely not home.

A few days later, my husband and I were having breakfast. Our daughter, then eight years old, joined us a few minutes later. She seemed disturbed. After a while, she told us, "I had a dream last night."

"What about darling?" I asked.

"I dreamt that Daddy died," she told us.

"That is not a nice dream darling," I said and looked across at my husband. He just smiled and continued eating.

Two weeks later on the 11th December 2006, our daughter, Martin, our foster son, and I travelled home to Rabaul for the Christmas holidays. Our twenty-five year old son had gone ahead two weeks earlier. As we were preparing to land at Tokua Airport, my mobile phone rang. I was stunned. We are always reminded to turn off our mobile phones before take-off. My daughter had switched off the phone. I saw her switch it off. It was my husband on the phone. I promised to call him as soon as we landed. I then turned to my daughter and asked, "Are you sure you turned off this phone?"

She replied. "I did Mummy."

So I then asked, "Then how come it rang just then?"

She shrugged and replied, "I do not know."

As soon as we landed, I called my husband from the airport public phone. I asked him if everything was alright. He said, "Yes everything is fine. I just wanted to spend some time talking to you." We had a long conversation before I got onto his Uncle's vehicle. He took us to our rented accommodation near to the place where one of my brothers worked. My brother is also accommodated there.

Two days later on Wednesday night, I felt so restless. I felt that I was being watched. When I woke up in the morning, my lips were swollen. Our son asked, "What happen to you Mum? Your lips look like a duck's bill."

"I must have been stung by some insect last night," I said. The swelling lasted two days.

On Friday morning, our daughter was restless. She wanted to speak with her father urgently. I promised her that we will call him on my brother's office phone. We would use our telephone card to call as soon as I was ready. I sent her ahead to my brother's house with her cousins.

I also had this urgent need to speak with my husband. I locked the door quickly and walked to my brother's house. As I was walking there, my mobile phone rang. It was my husband on the phone. He had never called so early in the morning whenever we were apart. He called to wish me happy wedding anniversary. I was so elated. We were married quietly in a Catholic convent chapel on the 15th of December, twenty-six years ago. He seemed so happy.

He then said, "By the way, your supervisor has sent feedback on your PhD thesis. I will save it onto my laptop and bring it home on Christmas". I was not prepared to work on my thesis during the Christmas vacation. I just wanted the family to spend some time together. He then asked for our daughter. I told him she had gone ahead to my brother's house. I asked him to call in ten minutes time. This gave me time to get to my brother's house to give the phone to our daughter.

When he called again, I gave the phone to our daughter. She was so happy to speak with her father. I heard her asked, "Daddy, when are you coming home?" I was not sure what his answer was, but my daughter said, "Daddy, I want you to come home now." She told him that she was playing with her piglet called Obelix. She gave the phone to me and my husband asked for our son. I told him he was still sleeping. I told him that we were preparing a special birthday dinner for Martin. He then said he had to get ready for work. He sounded different. His speech seemed blurred. I wondered if he had been drinking heavily the night before. I was so depressed.

Martin is an orphan. His father is one of my brothers. My brother died of liver cancer in September 2003. His wife, Martin's mother died in May, the same year. She died of a heart problem. I was reluctant to take Martin in because of extra expenses. My husband insisted that he would be better cared for if we took him as our own. I reluctantly agreed to take him in, on January, 2006. We did not know his birth date. When we asked when he was born, we were told he was born on the 15th of December 1999, the same day of the year as our wedding. My husband and I had looked at each other and smiled when we heard this. Martin had never had a birthday party so we decided to make this day special for him.

Everything was almost ready at 5.00 pm that day. My son, daughter, niece and nephews went to pick up the ice cream from the priest's freezer. I was helping my sister-in-law carry the food into the house. As I walked out of the house, I saw our son and daughter walking up with the ice cream, happily chatting with their cousins.

Then my mobile phone rang. It was my best friend calling from Port Moresby. I was so happy to hear from her. I said, "Sorry, we had no time to get together before we left, so you could dye my hair." There was dead silence. After a long pause she asked quietly, "Have you heard the news about your husband?"

I asked, "Is he alright?"

"No, I do not think he is," she replied.

"Was he involved in a car accident?" I asked.

"No. He had a heart attack. He is in hospital," she said.

"Is he alright," I asked again.

"No. I do not think so. I am going now to the hospital to check out this information"

I gave the phone to our son so she could speak to him. After their conversation he threw the phone on the grass and walked away. I was lost. I could not think. I began to cry when our daughter came to me. My brother comforted me. My sister-in-law organised the children to sit down to a quiet dinner. Martin's special day was forgotten.

I called my cousin and a colleague in Port Moresby to check out the news. I called my friend again for confirmation. She gave the phone to one of my husband's close colleagues so he could talk to me. He asked me where to take my husband's body. I replied, "The funeral home." I was so devastated.

I called my sister-in-law, an Air Niugini stewardess. She was also shocked. I asked her to organise for us to travel out of Rabaul on the first available flight the next day. This was quite challenging, given the Christmas peak period travel rush. We were wait-listed for travel the next day. At 10.00pm that night four names were deleted from the computer due to non- payment of fares. My two children, Martin and I were confirmed to travel back to Port Moresby at 4.30 am the next day. It was so amazing. We were able to return faster than normal.

My colleagues, cousin and sister were waiting for us at the airport. We drove to the funeral home. We found him sleeping peacefully. I noted a smile on his face as we stood around him. I still believed that he would wake up again. I felt for his heart eat. It was so still, so silent and so final.

Mystique Beauty/Queen of Grunge
By Ignatius Piakal

She had no name.

She drifted into view in all her unrestrained, radiant beauty that quiet Tuesday afternoon. She was clad in gear that could have easily passed for rags on anybody else, but it was simply haute couture on her.

As she stepped in, she removed a pair of aviator shades to reveal bright brown eyes that reminded me of sweet brown sugar at sunset. She perched them on a mass of lustrous black hair that had been pulled back in a bun, giving it an extra dash of sheen as if she needed any.

She had a don't-give-a-damn way about her in the way she carried herself as she drifted from one aisle to the next, momentarily pausing every so often to give an item a once over, and then moving on. Despite her seemingly nonchalant air, she moved with such grace with those well- toned limbs, she was pure majesty. She was slow-motion in real life. She was poetry in motion.

As she turned, you could just make out parts of a painted claw, reaching out for her neck from beneath the canvass of a tight-fitting Rip Curl t-shirt. The contrast enhanced a skin of flawless tone and texture. A pair of faded calf-length jeans hugged her hips down, the left leg folded up shin-high and righteously complemented with a pair of washed up Converse sneakers.

More golden brown of silky smoothness teasingly peered out from behind those jeans through silent tears where the majority of the cotton strands seemed to have surrendered to the abrasive demands of constant laundering.

After paying for her items she casually drifted into the liquor section and picked up a 12-pack Paradise white can, paid for it and made her exit.

Awed and intrigued by such careless beauty, I had to see how the story ended. Whether she got on her horse and rode out into the sunset or just disappeared into a tinted ride and into the arms of her Romeo.

But she was way too good for such cheap tricks. She stepped out and walked past every – mostly flashy looking – vehicle parked in the parking lot. Right at the end near the entrance was a beat up Land Cruiser, covered with caked mud and grime with two 44 gallon fuel drums at the back.

The entire setting was neatly complemented with three scruffy looking older gentlemen who were sitting at the back. As she approached, they clambered down and she handed them a few sticks of Spear cigarettes and a Ten Kina note for their buai. After helping themselves to it, two of them returned to their posts by the fuel drums and the oldest of the lot got into the passenger seat as the ignition kicked in with a turbo-charged growl.

They left soon after, leaving behind a smoke screen of diesel fumes which hung lazily in the air but for a few seconds.

That was the last I ever saw of her. I will probably never see her again. Perhaps she was just a figment of my imagination. She disappeared just the way she appeared.

She still had no name.

Dusk at Eriku
By Ignatius Piakal

A lone man walked hurriedly towards the bus stop at Eriku from the Morobe showgrounds as the sun was dipping low towards the west, the fading light slowly transforming the ancient rain trees on the golf course across the road into sinister shapes. Not a good time for anybody to be out and about around this side of town. Well, most of Lae for that matter – unfortunately.

Knowing this he picked up his beat double time from his usual pace. Despite his family's insistence to stay, he was obligated to his duty as a man of the cloth, and had to attend to a request from a church member who was gravely ill with malaria.

While keeping to the sidewalk, he looked up as his eyes darted from side to side, scanning the immediate horizon, concentrating especially on the figures milling around the Highlands Highway bus stop. From that distant he figured they most likely had to be late travellers.

Potential passengers waiting for that last tulait-tulait express – the late PMV buses that convoy out of Young Creek up the highway at midnight. This gave him just an ounce of faith, enough for comfort and the courage to brush aside his doubts and put his foot of 'faith' forward.

But as he got closer his heart sank as he realized his error in judgement. They were potential passengers alright; potential passengers for Kamkumung and Three-Mile and nowhere else. It was too late now to even consider the idea of switching into reverse gear. He hesitated but only in his mind because the last thing one would want to do in such a situation is to visibly display hesitation. Such actions to the eyes on the street would denote fear.

And on such a day fear is a very bad commodity to possess. Fear invites horror.

Maintaining his stride with a calm exterior, he silently muttered a prayer under his breath and pushed on with a straight face. The air was thick and sticky with the sickly smell of cannabis permeating all around as lazy bloodshot eyes lay their invisible grasp on him. Eyeing him.

Sizing him. Vultures picking their meal on a mad Friday at dusk.

As he walked past the bus-stop shelter, he noticed the din of raucous hyena laughter from the shabby looking bunch near the public toilets carried over more clearly this time than earlier.

At that instance he realized the truth behind this was because the crew of miscreants nearer to him had all fallen silent. No sooner had that realization hit him when the overpowering stench of cheap liquor hit his olfactory glands as a throng of rabid-looking, scruffy young men had him locked up in a human cage.

"This is it," he thought, as hands with no faces groped and ran over him and into his pockets and out of them, knowing where exactly to go as if they were on familiar turf. The knowledge struck him then that those hands had treaded similar roads a thousand times before on many unfortunate, weary souls like him. In this adrenaline powered confusion, a moment of crystalline clarity found him wondering what the fate of those faceless souls was like, and how their story ended.

Give ear,
For I hear
Crystal as clear,
Arise a cheer.
A cheer for fear.
Prepare a tear.
For I fear
That fear,
Again wins clear.

With these thoughts, the reservoir of fear locked up inside of him all this time just broke its dam, gushing through his entire being like a torrential rush in a relentless downpour. His mind in a last bid stand for reason told his body to brace itself for the quite call of the cold taste of steel. Or would it be loud? Would it be messy? Would there be many? How would he take the pain? Or will he even feel the pangs of this foreign invasion at all.

With his mind in a cyclonic state of rush, his voice simply keeled over, losing all its vocal ability to make even a squeak, much less a scream. So the heart stepped into the place of the larynx and screamed like mad inside his chest with the voice of his father's kundu drum.

Ka-tum! Ka-tum! Ka-tum!

And he remembered his Father.

"Father," he called out with a voice normally reserved for his dreams.

As if in response, a voice, markedly laced with urgency cut through the dying light of dusk and the nightmare that was.

"Hei bois, weit pastaim. Weit pastaim. "

"Dedi-Boss, osem wanem yah?" someone responded.

The man they called Dedi-Boss stepped closer, standing about 20 centimetres above most of this measly bunch, roughly pushed them aside and away from the pastor and indicated him with a nod and in the true spirit of a strit mangi drawled, "Husss...ehhhh. Mi save long em yah. Givim ol staf blo em bek na larim em go. Em bikpla mangi blo Jisas yah."

Relief hit the preacher man like a punch to the mid-section as he crumbled and fell, rushing into the black swirling arms of comforting darkness that reached out for him from somewhere beyond, enveloping him in black bliss.

Friends for Life
By Reginald Renagi

The first time this new girl joined my third grade class, I wanted to be her friend for life. I was smitten with Grace ever since her family moved next door to us. Grace and I attended the same primary "T" school in our small suburb. As close neighbours, we virtually grew up together through our school years. At the beginning of each year, Grace and I found ourselves in the same class.

One Friday afternoon, our fifth grade class was restless. We had worked hard on a new concept all week. I could sense that the other students were also edgy with one another. To relax, we played a little game. I asked Grace then for us to list on a blank paper something nice about each other and signed at the bottom, "Friends for Life". We would read it frequently and make a big joke of it. Grace treasured this list and neatly folded the papers to put them inside a small empty perfume bottle.

The years flew by fast and before I knew it, Grace was in my high school class again. We had by now developed a strong bond with each other and were now more than just friends. Soon, Grace and I completed our year ten with high marks, and left to pursue different challenges in life. We parted as good friends. It was the last time I would ever see Grace.

Thirty years passed and we lost contact for many reasons. It was six years ago after a trip abroad and my uncle met me at the airport. The drive home was quiet, each to his thoughts. Then my uncle cleared his throat.

"The Ralai family called last week and asked for you," "Gee, I haven't heard from them in years. I wonder how Grace is." My uncle said. "Grace died last Saturday." "The funeral is tomorrow, and her parents would like it if you could attend."

The funeral service was difficult for me. The pastor said the usual prayers. Grace looked very beautiful and appeared to be sleeping. I was the last one to bless her coffin and stood there awkwardly.

After the funeral, all of Grace's school friends (and mine too) headed to her parent's house for lunch. Grace's mother and father were there, obviously waiting for me. They asked me to remain behind as everyone left, one by one.

Grace's parents shared with me her personal photo albums. They had kept a good collection of family photographs of both of us from third grade to final year of schooling. I felt nostalgic.

"Before you go son; we want to show you something you should know that is very dear to Grace's heart". "We'd like you to meet our granddaughter, Evonne". I thought I was seeing double and that Grace has come back to life. Evonne's angelic face told me all I needed to know why Grace never mentioned her daughter to me in her letters all these years.

Grace's mother said, taking a small lady's wallet to show me. "We found this in Grace's tightly-clutched hand before she left us peacefully". Evonne started to speak.

"Mum told me everything and I can see why now". Her grandmother added, "We thought you might recognize this." She opened a plastic wrapping paper, and carefully removed two worn but neatly folded pieces of paper from a small perfume bottle.

I knew without looking that the papers were the ones on which Grace and I had both written in fifth-grade listing all the good things we liked about each other and signed our names together, "Friends for Life." Grace's mother said. "As you can see, our Grace treasured it for years until the end."

"Mum always carried this with her at all times," Evonne said to me without batting an eyelash. "She had this faraway look whenever she talked about her special friend. He was always there for her and how she wished he was by her side in her final days". A lump formed in my throat. "Mum told me who my real father is". I am glad you came. This was mum's last dying wish to know my father."

Evonne started to stutter and tremble. "Mum never stopped loving you". "Her only wish in life was to be able to hear you say that you loved her", the rest was lost in a mumble of incoherent words. I immediately extended my arms wide as she rushed to embrace me with an anguished cry.

That's when I finally broke down. I cried for Grace and for all the years I wasted pretending to hide my feelings for her because of my obligations, and the ties that I had. I cried for Evonne for denying her a chance to know me. But I cried now for my friend who I would never see again.

Evonne and I cried out loud our grief. "I am truly sorry my dear Evonne, please forgive me. Oh, darling Grace, you always knew that I loved you, but was afraid to tell you". Oh Grace, sobbing her name over and over in anguished lamentations to an empty room.

Evonne's grandparents discreetly left us to reconnect after so many years. It was a great healing feeling of self-discovery between father - and daughter of his first true love.

The good Lord has blessed my loss and Evonne would always remind me of Grace. Thank you my darling Grace, I have always been your friend for life!

The density of people in society is so thick that we forget that life will end one day. And we don't know when that one day will be. So tell those you do love and care about that they are special and important.

Tell them you loved them ... in the living years for it's too late to say sorry when we die.

"Do you have the ship, Navigator?" By Reginald Renagi

After a two-year training stint in Australia, my first sea patrol as a ship's third officer started off in typical fashion.

The Executive officer spoke into the ship's PA system: "Special Sea Duty men and Cable Party close up". "Assume damage control state 1, condition yankee!" "Single up all lines!"

"Let go all lines, all hands fall in for leaving harbour".

The Captain ordered: "Revolutions 650 Charge, Coxswain steer 085". "Navigator, take us out of harbour". "I answered Aye, Aye, Sir".

After leaving Seeadler Harbour and the Admiralty Group (Manus) over 48 hours earlier cruising at 12 and a half knots, the sleek fast Attack-Class patrol boat, HMAS AITAPE transited China Straits passing Samarai Island on her port beam enroute on a Westerly course for Port Moresby.

It was still pitch-black in the wheelhouse when I struggled up the ladder 20 minutes to the hour to relieve my captain from his middle-watch ("the guts" are from mid-night to 0400). The ship was being tossed about like a floating cock in a basin so that climbing up the stairs was a gymnastic feat in itself.

"Good morning Sir," saluting him. "Morning Nav" (short for Navigator). "Ready to take over?" "Ready when you are, Sir". The Captain went through the motions of handing over the watch to his third officer. The Officer-of-the-Watch (OOW) was doing the morning watch-handover in the small wheelhouse.

It was over in 20 minutes and before leaving to retire to his cabin below, the Captain appeared somewhat uncertain. I could sense this and said, "Go on Sir, it's been a tough watch and you do need to take a break. I'll be fine".

"Are you sure, Nav? This weather's rough as guts".

I grinned back saying, "She'll be right Sir and I've seen worse..." and did not finish as he appeared about to chuck all over the wheelhouse deck.

The captain appeared to have changed colour in the face. He hesitate as if about to change his mind on leaving a still inexperienced Officer of the Watch (OOW) on his own to make one last-minute reminder to his third officer.

"Well then number two (Navigator), remember, don't forget to call me as per my 'Captain's Night Orders' if you are in any doubt whatsoever. Is that clear?" "Aye Aye Sir." "Well then, that's it from me."

The morning watch weather was very rough. Amidst a cacophony of sounds, I barely heard the captain's voice as another loud crashing sound violently shook the small warship from stem to stern sending a series of never-ending vibrations throughout the ship. It's as if the small ship was about to break into many pieces as she rolled heavily on her side into the wave's deep trough.

I saluted; the skipper turned and was gone from sight, disappearing in the shadows down below. There would not be any sleep for the captain this morning.

As the ship's navigator, the lives of eighteen sailors rested entirely on me and my skills as the OOW for the next four hours of some of the roughest weather one can ever experience in our tropical waters.

I looked at the big sailor at the helm and ordered: "Steady," he immediately responded in the standard manner, "Steady on Two-seven zero degrees, Sir "(270). "Steer Two-Seven Zero (270), Steer Two-seven Zero (270)." "Course two-seven zero, Sir (270)." "Roger leading-hand" (acknowledging the response).

I continued on with my last conning order to the helmsman who by now was struggling to stay on the course given by the OOW in this wretched weather. His hands were gripping the spokes of the steering wheel so hard that I feared the steering linkages would snap under the strain.

"Look here sailor, I know it's hard on you, but we don't want to break the steering wheel so go easy on it. We will maintain this course as much as possible for the next hour. When we passed the Hood point light off our starboard beam, we will make a ten degree further change of course to 280 and hug the coast as much as possible in this weather until daybreak."

"Hot brew, Sir?" "Great stuff, and thank you, lookout" "Keep your weather eye peeled. We don't want to run into anything solid in this God-forsaken weather."

I was suddenly jolted back to the present by a big wave crashing down on the foredeck where the big 40-60 Bofors gun turret was situated.

It seemed to go on forever as I kept peering through the thick windscreen glass with its wipers going at full speed. "Another cup of brew, Sir?" "Yes, thanks." "The usual, Sir?" "No, coffee will do." "Standard navy brew, Sir?" "No, a little different this time." "How different Sir?" "Just like my woman?" "Pardon me, Sir?" "Sorry, make it black and strong, no sugar and milk, thank you." The chef flashed me a wide grin.

"And would you like your breakfast now too, Sir." "What's for breaky, chef?" "It's standard navy, Sir." "Oh, that's great!"

The chef disappeared aft into the small galley. Within seconds he was back and holding a huge plate. "Here you are, Sir." Breakfast for champions from the finest chef onboard! The plate was filled to the edges … bacon and eggs, poached, scrambled or fried sunny-side up, bangers, tomatoes, beetroot, fried onions, ham, pineapple slices and other stuff. "Why thank you chef, that's my favourite on the Stalwart!"

"I know Sir", and before I could ask him how he knew, the chef had already disappeared into the small galley where the familiar sweet aroma of coffee and fried eggs and bacon was coming through the galley-doors in the starboard passageway leading to the wheelhouse.

In another 20 minutes the lookout would pipe the 'Wakey Wakey' call throughout the ship calling all hands to breakfast.

I thought I was going to enjoy cruising the Papuan waters for the next 21 days…ah, what a life for a seafarer.

The Centenary Voyage
By Leonard Fong Roka

Akora was a Grade 11 student at Hutjena Secondary School. His slim build and weakling-like posture had many of his school mates concluding that was an explanation for his easy-going attitude to life. But when he felt like slopping over the brim of his self-contained world it was hard to understand the new side of his personality.

Nobody, not even his own folks from Kieta, knew whether he had a girl friend or not. It was hard to squeeze out his secrets—he was too stolid. He travelled to places that most Kietas feared. For his dreams and him nothing could come between.

The year 2011 was the hundredth year since Catholicism had landed in Bougainville. Jubilee celebration talks infiltrated every conversation in the school. Akora, although a Catholic and often attracted by the jubilee-related radio jingles, kept aloof for his own reasons.

Easterly and sea originating gusts of wind swept through the Hutjena Government Compound continuously harassing his reading. Intermittently, when the wind—with its ingrained cruelty—pitied him and abated, the loud sound of the singing by the practicing student choir in the mess hall took its turn to disturb his concentration.

"Hey, Tebu, ol wokim wanem long mess?" he asked his bunk mate making his ingress to Dorm 17.

"Aung, they are Catholics," Tebu answered, "practicing the centenary song. They'll be leaving on Thursday by ship for Tunuru in Kieta. Brother Joe from Hahela is conducting them."

Akora followed his mate into the dormitory and they sat lost in thought.

"Sans, mi lukim peles pinis,"Akora said, boastfully as he turned to a new page in the novel that he was reading, *Things Fall Apart* by the Nigerian author, Chinua Achebe.

"No. Aung, they are saying that only the ones involved in the rehearsals are going," a boy grooming himself in his bunk said with a laugh.

Akora, with his mind concentrated on the book, absent-mindedly joked, "Sir, those nice voices and that pes-meri conductor, if they happen to leave me here, they'll never get into Heaven. As for me, I'll be there with a carton of beer to party with my Lord. You know; I'll tell Him, Jesus, let's go back to the Cana days." They all laughed at the silly joke.

Days went by like the water in a river that has no resort to holidays. All the Kietas looked forward to a trip home in their centenary attire, if only to regain the smell of their so-missed home. From his distance Akora also shared with them that desire; that longing to be home.

Thursday found Akora very early in the dust and salt scented Buka township. Along the limestone gravel-covered streets Kietas wandered everywhere aimlessly. "So, you see, so many Kietas hiding in different corners of Buka island," he said to his friend and classmate, Barapa'nung.

"Masika'ra, era," Barapa'nung snuffled in the cloud of dust dragged along by a passing truck. "Many of them have never even felt a fine church pew even once." He paused to cross the road for the market, and then added, "Tonight, they'll all pack aboard the MV Sankamap for the joy of being seen in Tunuru as a bunch of faithful Catholics."

Akora reluctantly chuckled, "Aung, and what about us trying to get on board, have we any desire for fellowship with the church?"

"Always, we are." They laughed and entered the market.

Across the mighty and tenacious (if you fall into it) Buka Passage, the church chartered vessel was resting idly at Kokopau wharf, patiently waiting for the Tarlena Secondary students and others to embark.

In the background of the growing Kokopau station the coconut palms lining the high ridge above were swaying in the wind with absolute fidelity. Just like Buka, trails of dust were marking the whereabouts of moving vehicles.

At the northern entrance of Buka Passage, just outside Iata village, gulls fished in the glare of the setting sun on a calm sea besmirched by the pure whiteness of the remnants of crushing mighty waves in the area believed to be the spot where the flowing passage water meets the immobile ocean.

The take-off horn of the ship blared at half five toppling those twang-like piercing sounds of the few motor boats ferrying across the passage through its undulations and bulging waves. "Era, otherwise that thing leaves us here," complained Akora, his eyes staring at the black diesel fumes emanating from the ship's funnel in the distance.

The boys were intrigued and tucked into the last contents of their food parcels before dashing out of the market. "That ship must be coming here," Barapa'nung reasoned. As they wondered the school truck appeared in front of them. "There, you see, the students are here. They will be crossing the passage for the ship is coming to this side."

As they approached the wharf, the ship was there slowly engaging itself to the bridge.

"Anangka, de are kuada remang?" a wantok straying near the port gate asked them. "Students are inside the gate, are you two going with them? Will you be on the ship?"

"No, we are only going to the bank's ATM," they lied. "Not interested in Kieta girls; the Buka one's are getting sweeter every day, you know."

This was Akora's way of answering questions from strangers. He loved short, cryptic answers where the enquirer must work out the rest in his own mind.

A good number of the choir students called to them as they walked under the street lamps but they ignored them, pretending not to be interested in being homeward bound.

They headed towards the bank and sat there watching the mass of people sorting out their travel papers. Later on they moved under the mango tree in front of the port's main entry gate, to Akora a handy coign to keep an eye on developments.

The shrilling crickets annoyed them but they remained there calculating what steps they needed to take; one thing hindering them was the fact that neither had 15 kina to pay for the voyage to Kieta. Akora, however, had a plan.

"We'll go in there, together," Akora told his partner, "as we reach the money collector, I will send you back. That will give me time to play games with the cash-man, his receipt-boy and the person in the queue with me. Understood?"

"Yes!"

Strong gusts of wind were blowing litter everywhere. Leaves from the mango tree rained down on them. There were no twinkling stars high in the sky, just the powerful flash of lightning and the sound of thunder to the north. In the chilly air the boys marched towards the ship.

As they jostled through the crowd, an announcement was made, "All Hutjena students listen carefully as we read your names; when you hear your name cross the gang way. If your name is not called, you will have to pay K15 for a ticket."

As the list was read, the students snuggled into the floating house of the ship while the no-names began paying cash to Brother Joe, whose bald head, to Akora's amusement, glittered in the bright lighting of the ship. The boys approached him.

"And you two? Painim wanem, maski lo bihainim ol meri," Brother Joe, laughed. "Who is giving me K15?"

Akora watched Brother Joe write the receipts while the other brother, whom he was not sure about, collected the cash. Beside them, stood a couple of huge and aggressive looking security guards; the gangway was manned by them too.

"I will pay you," Akora said. "Barapa'nung just came to see me off." As an afterthought, he added, "Hey, Barapa'nung, my bag is there under the mango tree; go and fetch it."

"What were you doing under the mango tree?" Brother Joe asked, with a giggle.

"Just write me a receipt," Akora told him. Looking at the woman in the queue behind him he said, "Hey, woman pay money to the cashier and this pipia Brother will write you the receipt."

"Have you paid too?" Brother Joe asked him.

"You write my receipt and keep it there and I'll go and pay; you'd better write this woman her receipt as well."

Brother Joe did just that and Akora moved over to the cash collector and handed him some areca-nut and started a conversation. They chatted like old friends, occasionally getting the receipt-man involved. When he thought he had them in his trap he would go back to Brother Joe for his receipt and he was sure he wouldn't hesitate to hand it to him since he had been with the cash-man for some minutes. The timing was perfect and he presented himself to Brother Joe, again.

"My receipt, please?" he asked, confidently.

"Here you are, and safe trip, my pamuk boy."

As planned, Akora boarded the ship and then walked to the bow area and handed the ticket to Barapa'nung, who was, after a few minutes, safe onboard beside his partner. They relaxed and looked forward to the voyage ahead.

All this was done under the brewing storm. Then came the mooring lines, followed by the gearing up of the ship's engine, which felt like an earth tremor to Akora.

The ship steamed north towards the open sea and Kieta in pitch darkness, unsteadily hustling against the tormenting winds and gigantic waves.

Waves as high as Mount Takuang attacked the ship continuously, causing stifling discomfort for poor Akora who now thought of nothing but sea sickness. "We are entering the mouth of a devil storm, boy," Akora told Barapa'nung as they sat on the wet coaming canvas. "Let's go into one of the cabins."

Nobody was interested in exploring the warmness of the cabin with the waves hammering the vessel. Akora held tightly onto the canvas seam even though some stability had been gained and the floating house was churning on through the tempestuous sea. Fear gripped him yet.

To further add to their displeasure rain poured down in a torrent in collaboration with the cruelly rollicking wind hissing in the struts. Nobody was stable: people stood and then sat and uttered complaints or just wandered about, hands clutching at anything for balance—not even taking the chance to glimpse at the storm outside.

Akora lay prone on a bed offered to him by an old friend, Asino a student from Tarlena. He was sick in the belly. "You know, I felt awkward taking up this bed when other people needed it," Asino boasted in a distant murmur; but pain was permeating his bravado. "You are lucky—" The ship quaked and he too was dangling over the bed vomiting with heavy gasps. Somewhere a child was wailing in gulps too.

With his chin resting on his wrist Akora painfully scanned the room. Everywhere people vomited onto the metal floor. A few with a little strength left staggered outside but returned wet all over from the sea spray and rain. Occasionally people bumped into the rails or bed frames as the vessel jerked uncontrollably.

As he laid in discomfort, Akora chided himself for taking this journey. "Why did I take up this voyage," he murmured. The thought of jumping overboard momentarily occurred to him but he dismissed it quickly. "Get lost, he said." He prayed with the woman next to him. As he meditated he kept his eyes on his female neighbour. She was mumbling in dulcet tones with a rosary resting in her palms.

He initially eyed her quite cynically but then admonished himself. She was beautiful, like every student from Tarlena, especially now with that frightened look. Her hair was neatly braided and a white t-shirt covered her agile body.

Just then, a giant of a wave struck. The churning of the ship's engine wavered. The clock on the wall that was reading midnight was suddenly not there anymore. The ship jerked, bounced and then jerked again and again. Impetuous was its lurching.

Akora was not within his senses. In the darkness he attempted desperately to get to his feet but to no avail. He tried to scream but not a sound was uttered as the whole mass of the rosary girl, Jacklyn, was stuck to him. Her cheek blocked his mouth from calling while her bare thighs were all tangled up with his.

The smell of strong perfume overwhelmed him. Her warmth was erotic and liberating from the defiant storm outside. They both—now having each other for comfort—considered the dangers outside as a soothing lullaby for them—two desperate lovers.

Akora ran his palm down her smooth back and hesitantly under her panties. He began caressing her buttocks to no objection.

The darkness was prolonged due to some mechanical mischief in the ship's engine. With that blessing he straddled her and they made love as the terrified people around them, mindful only of their own survival, ignored them.

The morning sun caught them in separate beds as the ship slowly made its way into Loloho wharf. They eyed each other with affection and talked about the new place before them. Jacklyn was taken by the rugged mountains and giant boulders that reached high into the skies of Kieta and her brown eyes were wide.

White seagulls soared high in welcome. The green mountains and rolling hills, mottled here and there by huge white galip-nut tree trunks, were magnificence to the Petat's Island girl.

The ship docked carefully against the wharf and the lovers walked down the gangway laughing to themselves and discussing what had crept into their world.

"Aung, from which corner of Kieta do you come from?" Jacklyn asked shyly as they strolled in front of a bunch of curious on-lookers.

"Panguna is where you belong, rait lewa."

"Em orait tasol," she said proudly and hugged him before the dozens of wondering eyes.

Wawen Billy
By Gina Samar

"Aiyooooo ah, aiyoooo ah, papa blo mi ya ah ah ah," went the heart wrenching sobs as we approached Wawen Billy's house.

It was December 1992. I had just completed my first year of high school when Wawen Billy passed away in Port Moresby.

Wawen in my mother's Arapesh tongue refers to one's mother's brother. Billy was not only my mother's brother, he was her surrogate father. She often described him as the man she would go to when her pencil needed sharpening.

You see, back then, pencil sharpeners were few and far between. Pencils were sharpened with razor blades, preferably Dad's shaving blade. My grandfather was long gone by the time my mother required this service; in fact he had passed on shortly after my mother's birth. So while other children went to their dads to have their pencils sharpened off she would go to Wawen Billy.

As you can imagine, the period after Wawen Billy's death was a time of immense grief for my mother. Relatives and friends visited her, brought food and made monetary contributions.

When the decision was made to take Wawen Billy home we prepared for the journey. Wawen Billy's body was embalmed and we left Port Moresby for Wewak where we then travelled by road to But, his native village, the place where he was born, where he had lived and loved and now would be his final resting place.

The solemn procession of vehicles drove steadily with its grieving passengers and the coffin. We approached the seaside village, turned into the driveway that led into the main village area, headed towards Wawen Billy's house and that's when the wailing started.

It was my cousin Evelyn, Wawen Billy's daughter.

"Papa blo mi ya ah ah ah," her stomach heaved with sorrow.

And so we all began weeping for Wawen Billy who would never again set his eyes on the clear blue sea and the golden sand or feel the salty breeze and enjoy the warm sunshine.

Forgotten
By Bernard Sinai

I looked at the couple again. They looked completely in love, holding hands at the Down Town bus stop without a care in the world. The Port Moresby heat did not seem to bother them. I think they would have stayed there the whole day if they could. To the rest of Port Moresby's citizens, the heat and sun would have been compared to Hell but to them that spot where they sat was Paradise.

She looked in his eyes and smiled. It was a magical moment.

The guy was tall dark and had a shortly trimmed beard giving that rugged look. He was well built and masculine, and would have easily swept her off her feet with one hand. He looked at her and whispered something in her ear.

The arches of her back and shoulders presented a well-defined figure, and from the firmness of her muscle tone; she was definitely athletic, probably played netball or basketball. The edge of her t-shirt revealed a lightly tan creamy brown skin.

She turned and gave a beautiful smile – a smile that looked too familiar.

My heart skipped a beat and then resumed with an intense tempo. I felt my stomach clench and my palms started sweating. The soft gentle melody that had accompanied the image of the lovebirds now turned to an intense pulsating angry beat.

Sure enough, there she was smiling lovingly at someone that I hardly knew. She was giving him the same look she gave me when we first met.

Then, like the sudden illumination from a match stick in a dark room, everything became clear for a second and then faded away into the blackness. My head started to spin and I felt like vomiting as I digested the scene before me. My girlfriend was cheating on me and I had no idea. "That bitch!" I said angrily. She could have had the decency of telling me but instead she decided to treat me like a dog. As I started to think about it, the feeling of humiliation started to set in. How long had this been going on? How long had her friends known about this? And how long have I been playing the fool?

Piece by piece the puzzles started to fit and a picture started to emerge. It was the same guy she had been secretly texting late at night. She always maintained that she was texting a girlfriend or relative and being so gullible, I readily accepted every lie. How could I have been so blind? It was happening right before my eyes, the "working late" routine, "I'm at a friend's place" and all the other little excuses that she used to give were actually starting to make sense.

I stood up from the seat I was in and started to walk toward the bus door. As soon as I reached the exit, questions started forming in my mind "Why? Why go down there and make a fuss? Is it really worth it?" I turned back and sat right down. It was not worth it. There was no reason for me to go and start a fight - there was nothing worth fighting for. All my reasons for fighting had just walked away from me.

Off course, there was a fear of fighting in me. Everyone has that sometimes but why would I put myself in harm's way for someone who did not care about me. Would she have shed a tear if I was beaten? Would she have stayed by my bed if I was hospitalised? I doubt it. She probably would have helped her lover to attack me.

I turned and looked at her with a smile. I was angry but at the same overcome with a sense of relief. Destiny had a mind of its own and being together was not a part of that plan and it was better to find out sooner than later. It could have been worse. She did not see me. In fact, she was so into a world of her own that I doubt she would actually notice me if I stood a few metres away. As the bus started to proceed for 4 Mile, I put my hand out of the window and gave a last goodbye wave.

She saw me this time and looked up trying to figure the man waving to her. Her beau also turned. In an instant, that curious look turned to a frown and she turned away as if I was a stranger – I was already forgotten.

The Taming of the Tiger
By Bernard Sinai

The punch came at a high speed with force enough to make a hole through a brick wall. Everyone held their breath, knowing well what would happen to Ruby's beautiful face when the punch connected. For a moment, all that could be heard was the beating of hearts, drumming wildly with the fear of anticipation.

To everyone's amazement and relief, Ruby swerved and ducked to the right in such a way that she looked like a coconut swaying to the tune of the ocean breeze. Steve's mighty punch never connected. He had all his weight banked on this punch, hoping to give it maximum effect. But he never expected to miss, making him loose balance, and falling flat on his face.

In an instant, he stood up and glared at Ruby. His face twisted with shame, and his eyes wild with anger. He was now a wild beast with savage thoughts only of brutality and pain. He charged, roaring toward Ruby like a raging bull, placing his shoulder like a battering ram. But in his anger and haste he tripped and fell flat on his face again.

He jumped up reflexively as if he had fallen on glowing embers and shoved the kid next to him. He was now intoxicated with so much anger and shame, that his eyes turned bloodshot and his breath flared heavily like a foghorn warning of unseen danger. The veins on his forehead twitched and throbbed like it was ready to explode at any second.

Looking at his face, Ruby realised the imminent danger she was in and screamed, "Mommy! Mommy!" with all the sound her voice-box would muster. Her mother came out in a flash, an apron around her waist and a broom in her left hand looking like World War Three had just begun.

"Steve! What have you done to your sister now!?" these words came sweeping like an icy tempest, freezing Steve where he stood, unable to move. He looked like an angry, sweating elf that had just been turned into an ice statue by Snow Queen. His clenched fists slowly released but his eyes burned with rage. This burning rage was soon overcome with cold despair. Ruby was now under mother's protective net. He could not touch her now.

His eyes slowly filled with water. He turned and looked at the other kids with moist eyes. They all smiled. They were now liberated from his reign of terror. He turned and looked away as the water in his eyes overflowed and rolled down his cheeks, sagged on his chin, and then dripped to the ground.

The tiger had been tamed…for today.

The Dutiful Wife in an Unforgiving Society By Paul Waugla Drekore Wii

The early morning fog which hangs over Mondia Hill obscures her view of the small township of Kerowagi below.

Nancy Suaire walks carefully down the slippery track that leads to the main road - and the bus stop at Kerowagi station. A few paces in front is Tobias Dinanem, her husband of two years.

He walks boldly and confidently despite the mud and dirt covering his stockman's boots to the brim; and despite the slippery track they tread.

From time to time Tobias turns a corner and disappears from her sight, or his figure is obscured by the early morning fog which hangs low on the ground. Nancy walks faster to keep pace with him.

She is walking faster now. Nancy sees Tobias Dinanem a few meters in front. She imagines what might be evident on his face. He is determined to get to the Kundiawa airport on time for the 10:30 flight to Port Moresby.

"He might not be coming back for a whole year or two," she speculates as she trudges behind.

Uneasy thoughts burden her. 'Teine and Tom might come and take the two piglets. I am only a woman. I'm not strong enough to stop them."

Tobias' younger brothers took to marijuana and home-brew five years ago. They are incapable of living a decent village life, let alone sustain themselves.

The roar of automobile engines signals that Nancy and her husband are closing on the main road at Kerowagi station. She edges along behind, as a dutiful Kuman wife must do. As she walks, her heart aches. She knows with each passing moment that her husband is closer to being gone.

He will be separated from her physically and spiritually. Her husband is going to Moresby, a place Nancy has never seen in 22 years of existence. She contemplates life in the village without a husband and the many challenges that she must endure alone … without him. Her heart becomes even more embittered by the thought.

There is a crowd of people at the bus stop. Tobias Dinamen and Nancy wait in tense anticipation. A coaster bus stops right beside them. It is time to leave. Tobias looks at Nancy and she looks at him. He extends a hand. He longs to hug and embrace her and to tell her that he will come back as soon as he can.

She takes her husband's hand in hers and they shake hands. She knows that Tobias could not hug and kiss her at the Kerowagi bus stop.

Nancy steps back as the "boss crew" pulls the door shut and the bus moves away. She walks into the throng to let the broken heartedness dissipate. She understands she is a woman whose favour, and her people's favour, has been gained by a large sum of money as bride price.

She must remain dutiful to her husband, whether she is with him or without him.

She is enraged by the realization that she is left with no choice but to face the challenges of living in the village alone.

A dutiful Kuman wife contending with the hardships until her husband returns from the city.

"I call him Daddy" By Imelda Yabara

She stretched up as far as she could on tiptoes, for the Big Boy chewing gum at the top of the PK stand. Her two sizes too small jeans left red welts on her belly while her top strained against her upper arms and belly. The plaits in her hair were coming out and in tangles. Her t-shirt stained with today's breakfast and possibly yesterday's dinner.

She tugged on the t-shirt of the man who stood in front of her. Without turning, he slapped her hand away and straightened his t-shirt. She opened her palm and looked at the heap of coins that lay in it.

Sally reached out and touched her shoulder then pointed to the box of Big Boy chewing gum. Her little brown eyes followed Sally's finger, she nodded and said, "Can't reach it."

The man moved ahead, tapping his fingers on the counter as the shop assistant packed the groceries. The woman at the cash register managed a tight grimace like smile when she saw the child.

Sally took 2 packets down and took a coin at a time out of the child's palm placing them on the counter until she reached .80t.

"Who's that man?" Sally asked her.

"Uncle," she replied as she unwrapped her chewing gum with grubby little hands. The underneath of her fingernails black.

Just then someone brushed past Sally and slapped two kilos of mince-meat on the counter.

"Ruth, dear come here," her uncle suddenly called out endearingly. Beaming, Ruth bounced over to him, in her place stood a bigger version of her. Her chunky jewelry attracting envious stares while Chanel No 5 teased the nostrils of those around her.

Big Ruth beamed at Ruth's uncle as she paid for the meat. They walked out hand in hand, free hands carrying the plastic bags of groceries while Ruth ran after them.

When she reached the exit door she turned and waved before dodging an incoming person and running after the two, straight past an oncoming vehicle which screeched to a halt.

Sally watched unable to breathe.

"Inap long lukluk na tingim ol kustoma," snapped the lady behind the cash register.

A year later, while Sally was placing new stock in the coke fridges before the counter she felt a small tug on her meri-blouse, looking down she saw Ruth. Ruth had grown slightly taller. She had on a school uniform which hung off her shoulders like it was on a coat hanger. Her hair combed and plaited, her face, clothes' and fingernails were clean. Sally's arms itched to reach out and hug her.

"Aunty, can you get me that Big Boy," Ruth asked pointing to the top of the lollipop stand. As Sally reached up, out of the corner of her eye, she saw a hand grab Ruth and yank her out of her line of sight. Looking across she saw someone else pulling Ruth towards the next counter.

"Don't talk to strangers," he berated her as Ruth leaned back twisting her wrist in circles, trying to wrench her hand out of his grasp.

"I told you if you want anything, anything at all just ask me and I'll get it for you," he growled through gritted teeth.

He reached for a lollipop and thrust it towards her. Ruth stepped back, looked away. She shoved her hands behind her back. Once again Big Ruth breezed in.

"Ruth, get that lollipop and stop being difficult," she barked. Ruth stood behind her dodging the hands of the man who was reaching around Big Ruth attempting to grab her.

Big Ruth began placing the shopping on the counter and was in the midst of telling the man that there was no sugar when Ruth looked over at Sally, pointing at the man she hissed, "He's HER friend."

The man ignored Big Ruth, glared at Sally, before reaching around and yanked Ruth over to him. He picked her up then the lollipop and offered it to her. She shuddered. Big Ruth she smiled sweetly at the man while she pinched Ruth on the back. The man walked out carrying Ruth leaving Big Ruth struggling with the groceries.

As they neared the door Ruth glanced back over the man's shoulder holding Sally's gaze until she was out of sight.

Several months later they met again.

"Hello Ruth."

"Hello Aunty," Ruth replied.

"Long time no see," Sally said to the beaming child.

"Ian," said the man with Ruth as he reached out to shake her hand.

"Sally, nice to meet you," Sally replied.

"Are you a friend of Ruth's mother?" Ian asked.

"No," Sally answered, "Ruth and I are old shopping buddies."

His grin seemed to make his face glow. "I'd love to hear that story someday," he told Ruth who grinned back.

Ian turned to the counter and took down a packet of Big Boy chewing gum from the PK stand and put it down on the counter before unloading the rest of the shopping in the trolley.

Sally looked down at Ruth. She could only see gleaming white teeth as her small face stretched to contain the smile. Ruth reached up and pulled Sally down and said ever so quietly, "he's Mom's boyfriend, but I call him Daddy."

The Box
By Imelda Yabara

"Why na yu toromoi olsem? Longlong!" came the roar, followed by pummelling fists.

"Aaaaya yu orait ohhh…." the man said as he turned wide-eyed towards his attacker, a graying middle-aged woman.

"Mum…mum..MUMMY yu toromoi ya! Em wokim wok bilong em," Ruth said. "Sori papa baim long em," she explained to the man who stood gawking at his attacker who was now attempting to retrieve the pieces of the glass box by digging through the back of rubbish truck.

"It's just a box," he muttered.

"It's not just a box," the woman snapped. "Man bilong mi baim long mi."

"Na why na u toromoi?" the man asked throwing his hands up in the air.

"It fell down and broke and I tried to fix it with Super Glue but it no longer looks like it used too," the lady croaked, sniffling and wiping red rimmed eyes with the back of her hand.

"Come on, Mum, lets go," Ruth said gently steering her sniveling mother away from the curb and back into their home.

"Mummy, I can't believe you still have this," yelled Karen, Ruth's younger sister, from their mother's bedroom.

"Have what?" Ruth called back.

"This photo of Scampy. You know our first dog," Karen replied.

"Don't you touch anything on that table," their mother screeched before tearing into her room.

"Where did you pick it up from," Ruth asked the sixteen-year-old who was holding the photo up high so her mother couldn't reach it.

Karen pointed to the table with her free hand while the other still held the photo out of reach.

"I put everything that was in the box on the dresser. They're special keepsakes. Here...this coral I picked up during a walk on the beach the first time I went home to your father's village." their mother said.

"Oh…remember this Ruth," she walked over and held up a multi-colored straw necklace and looked at Ruth who shook her head. "It's the first thing you ever made for me. You made it several days after starting elementary school." She paused and laid it tenderly down on the table. "And these baby gloves are yours Karen, my mother bought them for you."

"What are the keys for?" Ruth asked pointing to a set of keys on the table.

"Oh those are the spare keys from the first flat your dad and I ever lived in. I told the landlord I lost them so I could keep them. When I threw out the box I couldn't find any place to put them. But how could that guy have just picked it up like that and thrown it into the truck. Did you see how it broke into pieces? I've…I've had it for 19 years," she whispered while touching the items on the table. The sisters stared at their snivelling mother stroking the objects then pausing every now and then to wipe a tear away with the back of her palm.

"I've got an idea," Karen blurted out running out and returning a few minutes later with three photo frames.

She began to remove a photo when her mother grabbed her hands. "No Karen, those are pictures of you and your father."

"It's okay mum…I know what I am doing," Karen told her.

Karen placed the photo of Scampy in one frame. The mitts in another and the straw necklace in last frame then propped them up on the table.

"Well that's taken care off. What about the keys and the coral?" Ruth asked.

A horn honked outside.

"It's daddy. Are you going to be okay by yourself this weekend?" Ruth asked their mother.

She nodded and wiped the tears and blowing her nose with some tissue from the tissue box on the dresser. She stood and straightened her meri blouse before looking in the mirror and patting her afro down.

"Go get your bags, your father is waiting," she told them.

She grabbed the keys and piece of coral then walked slowly out to the front door pausing to take a deep breath before slowly opening the front door.

"Hello Jack," she greeted him. She stood tall and clasped her trembling hands behind her back.

"Are the girls ready? I'm running behind schedule," he snapped drumming his fingers on the door of the car.

"They're coming," she answered. "Would you like to come in?"

"Naaa, I have to buy dinner so I'm just gonna pick up the girls and go," he told her.

"RUTH, KAREN hurry up," he bellowed before tooting the horn again.

Karen pushed past her mother before turning and throwing her arms around her.

When Karen moved away, Ruth walked past her took two steps then stopped and turned.

"Mummy," she said quietly.

"Yes dear what is it?"

"I was thinking you know someday you're going to find something else to put on the bedroom table so it won't feel like something is missing and you can collect new keepsakes."

"We'll help you look," Karen chimed in from the back of Ruth.

Miriam looked away. "On Monday" she rasped as she nodded to the hibiscus hedge that surrounded their home.

"On Monday then," Ruth repeated before the two sisters hopped into their father's BMW.

"So what are you starting on Monday?" their father asked as he reversed the car out of the driveway.

"Girl's stuff," Karen replied as she and Ruth watched their mother throw the coral and a set of keys into the now empty rubbish bin.

Who Got Custody of Dorigi's Soul?
By Tanya Zeriga-Alone

The appointment with death will happen for each human sooner or later, and for Dorigi, his was scheduled for one stormy night. That fateful night approached from the east on the wings of the thunder storm forcing the last rays of sun to concede a fast retreat across the sea and over the horizon. In his small hut beside the main family dwelling, Dorigi was drifting in and out of restless sleep. Beside him, his 250 watt battery powered lamp valiantly kept the fingers of the dark at bay. For Dorigi, the day was over, he was doing his home run after 83 long years of living and after ten offspring from the vigour of his youth, 30 grand offspring and an increasing number of great grand offspring. By the local standard, Dorigi had done well, he had been successful in multiplying his superior genes, but importantly, he had accomplished the mission of his life.

But the home run was a solitary journey. Just like in his mother's womb 83 years ago, his world was once again dimly cocooned in his mosquito net in his little hut, his world already grey from the losing battle with cataract in both eyes; his ears uninterested in the muffled conversations from the family hearth. His dehydrated skin was cool and dry like moulted snake skin hanging limp from his bony frame. His awareness of life was measured by the pain in his bones; pain even his mattress could not cushion.

The home run was also a waiting game, waiting for the darkness to close in, waiting for his heart to cease beating. The wait was also a time of reckoning. As a young man in his time, Dorigi was tall and solidly built and fearless like leaders of old who commandeered attention through their physical presence at tribal councils. Dorigi was touted to be one such leader and was mentored accordingly to carry on the secrets of his clan; secrets of hunting, secrets of sorcery - secrets zealously guarded by the headman of his clan.

At that point in Dorigi's life, a new influence was also infiltrating his tribal land. A carpenter from the tribe of Judah was recruiting men to become fishermen. The carpenter was giving men power over the spoken word and was sending them out as fishermen - not for fish but for human souls. Dorigi turned down the offer of the seat in the tribal council, and chose to follow the Jewish carpenter whose reward for collecting human souls was a promise – a promise of eternal life and a big house in an undetermined location. It was a challenging life trawling for souls, but the alluring promise of life everlasting and a big house kept Dorigi going and that was how he spent the prime of his life.

Fast forward time and here he was, cocooned in his darkened hut, a frail bag of bones but a proud one. His bony chest lined with invisible medals collected from the many human souls he had caught. His hope was now on the promise of a big house and a new lease on life, where his bones and muscles would be made vibrant again. Visions of dramatic exits on chariots of fire flashed before his eyes, dreams of vanishing into thin air, like in the stories of the faithful gone before him filled his imagination. The pain in his bones, however, brought him back to reality, robbing him of the escape his fantasy presented. Words from his tribal mentors could not stop playing in his head. Under the cover of darkness, he had been told, the spirits of those gone ahead come to get the souls of those made unwary by old age or illness and to entice those undecided between the world of the living and the dead. Every soul must then stand before the tribal council to be judged for a place in the big village.

The beginning of the end for Dorigi started early that evening. That evening air was motionless yet charged with electricity from the approaching thunder storm. Anxious mothers gathered their family together and prepared for an early night. After the evening meal while younger people crawled to bed, the older folks, who had lived through numerous births and deaths, stared into the dying embers of the fire and wondered if the approaching storm was a thousand warriors coming to take their reluctant souls to the tribal council. The approaching storm flashed lighting after lightning, painting flickering paths over the sea, paving the way for the accompanying rumbles of thunder. After a while, the storm reached land, lightning's flashed and thunders boomed and the wind mercilessly shook fragile shacks at their wooden foundations. Meanwhile, back in his hut, Dorigi ran a very high fever, his body was parched; his whole being craved water - delicious, cooling, thirst quenching water so abundantly flowing all around his little hut. He tossed and turned and squirmed as much as his stiff joints could allow him. He rasped out indistinct words through cracked lips, pleading release from his burning carcass, pleading for merciful water to carry him to blessed rest. After a while Dorigi calmed down into an erratic sleep, and as the vestiges of the storm accompanied the night in its last lap into dawn, the end happened for Dorigi - he exhaled his last breath from his dehydrated lips.

The rain had petered out, the wind had calmed down and the electricity of the storm discharged, when the rooster crowed its first watch. The death wail shortly after that from Dorigi's hut confirmed that a passing over had taken place during the storm. Older people who survived the night swore on the graves of their fathers that they heard the echo of conch shell in the early hours of the morning. Was it a conch shell summoning the prodigal son to appear before the tribal council? It could also have been a welcome trumpet into a new life. It remains a secret of the night as to who finally got custody of Dorigi's soul.

The Curse of Paranoia
By Tanya Zeriga-Alone

Even a serene night, softly illuminated by the glowing moon, gently caressed by the cool breeze with cicada serenades could not draw Eware out of his house; night time was a prison for Eware, until the first light of dawn. Even then, the light of day had its own restrictions on Eware's life. He was very careful with his habits - his food scraps, he put away carefully, his rubbish thrown away immediately into the sea. He ensured he got his betel nut and mustard himself. His lime he shared with no one. When he chewed betel nut, he would spray the spittle into fine droplets that got blown away with the wind. Spitting was just too dangerous. In his waking hours, his bilum would hang around his neck; at night his bilum became his pillow in case someone sneaked something into it or removed anything from it. Eware trusted no one.

Eware had all the reasons to be very careful. The quality of his life had deteriorated since he got rid of Sapa, his first wife and married Dona his second wife. The downward spiralling did not stop after Dona died and he acquired a third woman. Moe, his third wife deserted him at the same time that the village people disowned him. Even his sons turned their backs on him.

Eware had an idea about the source of all his problems. At the time when Dona was pregnant with his fifth child, he had caught Sapa lurking in his backyard. When confronted, Eware was sure he saw a sly smirk on Sapa's face when she responded that she was only checking out some betel nut palms she had planted previously. Eware had shamed Sapa's family when he sent Sapa back to her father's house. But he had only practiced his rights because Sapa had failed to give him any children. It seemed that Sapa was out to make him pay for his action. He believed she had put a curse on him.

Dona was a spinster, a distant cousin from his father's side – such a marriage arrangement was possible within Eware's matrilineal customs. Despite her homeliness, Dona had the virtues of a prized wife; she made big gardens and tended Eware's pigs and, most importantly, she bore Eware children. The children had come as a flood as if to compensate Eware for the childless years gone by.

At the same time, the floodgate of misfortune was unleashed on Eware's life. Dona died after the bloody and painful ordeal of birthing his fifth offspring – a breech birth. Eware lost the person who could make gardens to feed his brood and his pigs. Dona had not even borne him a girl child. The value of daughters was in the dowry from their marriage - a good marriage would also bring Eware status and rights to new garden land. A daughter would look after him in his old age.

Eware's third marriage ended when Johnny, Eware's first son, staggered home and died in his arms from respiratory complications.

Johnny was the first born, he ran away from home because he was stifled by his father's obsession with the notion that his family was cursed. Johnny and his brothers were forbidden by their father from mingling with the villagers for fear of bad things happening to them.

Johnny ran away from his restricted life to freedom in town. Eventually he got employment at the town forestry nursery - sieving soil all day long. He built himself a cardboard shack at the edge of the nursery and that was where he got acquainted with Julie. Julie and her friends were always available whenever Johnny and the other nursery boys had money to pay for some frolicking. Apart from sharing their bodies, the girls freely shared the dreaded human immunodeficiency virus. The virus rapidly reduced Johnny's immune system, which was already stressed from the chronic bronchitis that he had developed since he started work in the nursery.

When Johnny returned home, as scrawny as a chicken, the village people turned their backs on Eware; so did his third wife. Eware dreaded and loathed what his son had become but still he could not escape the tender feelings he had for his first born. Johnny died in Eware's arms alone and was buried in a shallow grave next to Dona.

After the passing of his son Eware sank into depression. The feeling of loneliness, hopelessness and worthlessness overwhelmed him. All his family and friends had deserted him - he had nothing to live for. He had no freedom for it was tiring to be constantly on guard for his life. He decided at that point that he would end his tormented life, but not before making Sapa and her family pay for his damned life. So he planned his payback.

That fateful night, Eware could not sleep, so he kept watch until the early hours of the morning. It was the time of the morning that even dogs fall into deep sleep. While humans and dogs slept Eware collected the dried coconut frond torch he had made and silently braved the darkness down to Sapa's hamlet.

Standing next to the first house in the hamlet he lit the coconut frond and lifted the burning torch to the thatched roof. The flickering flames encouraged by the morning breeze eagerly fed on the dry sago thatch and instantly grew into a hungry, devouring monster. Within seconds, burning pieces of thatch alighted on a second house and then the next. The whole village awoke to a jumble of confusion as three burning houses became one big inferno.

Meanwhile, Eware had become a possessed man – silhouetted by the light of the burning houses, he danced and celebrated his revenge. He was in his own world, oblivious to the pandemonium he had caused and he did not see the barbed spear hurtling toward him. The spear made contact with his chest; the force of impact lifted him off his feet and slammed him to the ground. The spear hit him just above his heart, severing a big vein.

The village was in chaos as the sun peeked over the horizon; women loudly mourning the two people taken in the blaze, children howling after their mothers, dogs yowling at the bedlam while men stood around the smouldering houses, shaking their heads and wondering why a recluse like Eware could inflict such violence on his ex-wife's family. Nobody paid any attention to Eware's gurgled mutterings as he choked on his own blood, but nothing really mattered to Eware – he had avenged the death of his loved ones and he was free, free at last from the curse.

POETRY

For Our Independence
By Hinelou Nini Costigan

36 years to make our mark
36 years we failed to start
At first glance that's what we see
except when I look at you I see me
I see children of all ages, children brought here through different stages
I see the children of Papua New Guinea
I see the band aid to soothe and remedy

Serenity is my home
The island in the sun
Sun rising, flowers in bloom, children laughing etc
The Chauka singing to God
Waves crashing, curving, bowing
Yes sir, serenity is my home

I'm sitting on a beach peacefully
While others strive for peace
How can we both be sharing the same lives
Upon this subtle violent earth?
How can we not question
two different extremes from birth?

I'm asking you oh PNG
What is your quest for life?
Because we have a day more to live
while others fight the knife!

I'm asking you oh PNG
How can we not feel pain?

While all brothers and sisters
Ultimately suffer shame

I'm asking you oh PNG
when will you start to learn?
That we are the ones with everything
All that others have only to yearn

I'm asking you oh PNG
Not to give up the fight
For gallant soldiers we may be
When we survive the night
I'm telling you Oh PNG
That I love you too damn much
But you have no clue how tough it is in the exterior out of home
So please grow, learn, succeed and give
So all our seeds can be sown.

Fear Rules the Roost
By Hinelou Nini Costigan

I'm afraid of gentle whispers
Afraid of soothing hugs
Afraid of genuine kisses
And looks of yearning love
I can't explain my fear
Only that it oppresses all
And I'm scared that if I drop
You won't catch me as I fall
Afraid I am of so many things, things I can't explain
Only that I woke one day
And felt fear derived from pain
I'm sorry that it's made me
And stuffed up with my mind

And I'm sorry that I don't have guts
To walk the dotted line!

Advice from a Warrior
By Jimmy Drekore

My father took the shield
I ran beside him
When arrows came I ducked
I looked at him

"wana elge pikra"
Son don't go too far
"bi panamia",
" kanre pa"
There'll be ambush
Careful, don't push
"Nenma unawa kanre"
"Kuman meklanna"
When your fathers are here
You'll step closer
"Nene hone pikra"
Never go alone
Son, don't go too far
They'll be ambush
Careful, don't push
When your fathers are here
You'll step closer
Never go alone

Those words guided me
Those words protected me
Those words saved me
Those words initiated me

I learnt this valuable lesson
Take advice and follow instruction
You'll become a man

Walking Barefoot to be Educated
By Jimmy Drekore

Quick little steps
Closing little gaps
We walked together
Walking bare footed
To be educated

School was far away
We were on our way
Walking bare footed
To be educated

We shared breakfast
We walked really fast
Walking bare footed
To be educated

One time we came late
Strolling through the gate
We were at the door
Eyes on the floor
We stayed together
He looked at us
With a strong voice he told us
We would be punished together
We came bare footed
To be educated

Other time scissors in his hands
We had no chance
Airstrip on our head
We felt really bad
We stood together
We came bare footed
To be educated

One cold morning
It was pouring
We came late again
We couldn't bargain
Meter ruler in his hands
We had no chance
Hit him on the head
Hit me on my head
Our tears fell together
We came bare footed
To be educated

Blest with a Burden
By Jeffrey Febi

The birds chirped a strange high tone
And danced to a new excitement
Something different is in the morning air
And nature sensed its essence

As you woke up to your daily chores
A smile you wore; it was differently calm
Not deceptive enough to hide your joy
But charming enough to enlighten your soul
To glimpse your life's finest moment

But the morning peace will be shattered

When the dawn of restlessness appear
To burden you in nine moons of trials
With tire and aches, stress and tears

And your soul will stir up moods
To calm a turbulent throat
In the heat of the day
To caress your weary limbs
In the silence of the night
To relieve the back off pain
In the freshness of the morning
To appease an annoying bladder

Rest you will need; oh sleep in peace!
And when you feel life's motions within
Hal--le--lu--ia!
In joy dream pleasant dreams
To the moon cast a bright smile
At dawn join the birds in choir
And yell the sun to hurry its lazy bum
For restless nights must make haste

And when your last moan resounds
(Phew!)
Whisper peace so the world would know
Your bundle of joy will take its place
To sing to your heart a new tune
Thank the birds your companions
Toast to the moon your guardian
And rebuke not the sun
For strength it will give

Aha! In His house let the priest know
You were blest with a burden

My Grandfather's Bilum
By Jeffrey Febi

How grandfather's bilum, which
Across my father's bare chest,
In a loving embrace sling.
Like the Leleki baskets' blest
How while so pregnant swing.

How dwelleth he my father in its rich
Splendour till handing-over of its rest,
Then over my clothed chest sways.
O this old bilum! like all other blest
No longer is laden with in my days.

For its treasures I search in earnest,
That I may grandfather's mind know.
O this bilum is no longer pregnant!
Along the way, maybe some time ago,
How many treasures fade; this instant

Till my sleep, I'll summon eagerness
To my modern soul strengthened to seek.
Grandfather's treasures may be hidden;
Yet thru a new eye must I ever peek
For glimpses my days have forbidden.

The Rising Wolf in the East
By Francis Hualupmomi

From the East lies the Wolf in a world of rational animal governed by the
"Law of jungle "
Once humiliated, defeated and ashamed by western kingdom aliens
Now the sleeping Wolf has awoken, reimaging itself, legitimizing its

leadership over the world of sheep
The Western kingdom under the lion is disturbed by its sudden rise
Will wolf threaten Lion's Kingdom?
Will Wolf be benign or benevolent?
Will Wolf assume leadership with its own Middle Kingdom?
One wonders if it is a return to tributary system in the jungle or
Peloponnesian war of jungle!

Oh My Penge
By Michael Dom

Oh my Penge
What a precious fool you are
to sell yourself so cheaply
Where is your forefather's legacy?
Your gardens, long unattended
are barren and overgrown in weeds
Our land that sustained
a hundred generations
lies pilfered, plundered and polluted
Grieve now for what you have done
more so what you have not
Give back to your descendants
what your ancestors gave to theirs.
Once upon a time
from a revered hilltop
you raised our beloved Kumul
so highly, proudly
proclaimed: identity and liberty
But you have swapped
our people's philosophy
for wealth and prosperity
A puffed ego and procured status
adorned with bright trinkets

as your shining vanity
yet stumbling like a clown
because caring less for caution
you have chosen an unenlightened path.

Oh My Penge
What a shameless fool you are
to submit yourself so basely
How many able men will labour for you
and how many proud women
will cradle your babies?

When your sons no longer bring you
your carved walking stick
you will lie in the ruins of your hausman
in cold grey ashes and sackcloth
lamenting your misery and loss.
When your daughters have all fled
to foreign tribes, as unpaid brides
or refugees of your savagery
none will return to bake kaukau
at your hearth, nor bring water
to quench your thirst
Thus you will choke
on stale memories of bygone years.

At your last and final repose
with no women to wail, nor kin to console
nor chiefs to kill pigs in your honor
your garden lands will be denuded
divided among your rivals
while your untutored children
will enter into bondage
to ignobility and shame.

Oh my Penge

What an insufferable fool you are
to sully yourself so ignorantly
How many good people
must endure you?

Waiting for Kadesh
By Michael Dom

Kadesh, we are waiting for you
Your first breath will be our sweetest memory
Your first footsteps will be an adventure into our life
We will give to you everything that we are
Our hopes will be your certainty
Our dreams will become your reality
Your aspirations will be our fantasy
Your life will become our eternity
When your hands reach to touch
You will first have us to hold
When you cry at night, we will hear you
When you awaken, we will be watching
We will comfort you when the thunder rolls
We will succour you when the night falls
We will love you with the passion from which you were born
Will you be bold? Are you not already in our hearts?
Will you be beautiful? Are you not already so?
You are for us, fulfilment in a hollow world
Where peace is more oft lost than found
And so much hatred and fear abounds
All we ever have against this is love
Our love, which you will evidence
Kadesh, we are waiting for you.

PNG Flag
By Janice Isu

Paradise bird,
snuggle near
to the Southern Cross
lay you both down
embed in red
and black.

Children of PNG,
People of my land,
Behold….our flag!

Us, in all our
diversity.

Our identity,
our destiny.
The symbol
of our land.

The voice that
proclaims
our freedom,
declaring
our Nationality.

Soar higher
Paradise Bird,
spread your wings
and fly,
raise that

banner of hope,
for the future
generation.
Lest they
forget, all
you represent.

PM's Sandal Incident
By Janice Isu

Unstrap my sandals
Strip me naked,
If you dare!
Stand will I still.

Tie me up
if you must,
hope you keep
me down.
for I've got bones
made of stone,
and you can't
keep me bound.

Make of me
a public spectacle,
sound the alarm
I'm no terrorist.

I'm a man
of deeper roots
the Father
of a nation,
independent and free

like the wind
that ruffles the waves

a strategic nation
causing tidal waves
a bird with flamboyant
colours,
akin to the rainbow
a promise in the sky
always bound to fly
watch me rise
one more time.

The Big Man
By David Kitchnoge

The great warrior
The protective barrier
Was my big man
The mighty hunter
The famine buster
Was my big man
The grand gardener
The feast maker
Was my big man
The powerful orator
The freedom fighter
Was my big man
The magic maker
The awe inspirer
Was my big man
The splendid dancer
The joy bringer
Was my big man

The well dressed
The cash drenched
Is my big man
The pot bellied
The master bully
Is my big man

The Price of Indifference
By David Kitchnoge

I heard her cry
She'd lost her child
But I didn't bother
She wasn't my child
I saw her begging
She wasn't educated
But I didn't bother
She wasn't my child
I saw her being robbed
She was vulnerable
But I didn't bother
She wasn't my child
I heard him swear
She was being abused
But I didn't bother
She wasn't my child
I lost her today
She was stabbed
And I made a fuss
She was mine
I pleaded for support
She was precious
But no one bothered
She wasn't their child.

This New Way
By Lapieh Landu

This new way is
Whiteman's way
Throw away your digging stick
Here, take my shiny shovel
This new way is
Whiteman's way
Do away with your tiny shells
Here, take my silver coin
This new way is
Whiteman's way
Forget your wantok
Here, take my fellow dim dim
This new way is
Whiteman's way
Dispose of your slimy sago
Here, take my sweet white grains
This new way is
Whiteman's way
Be naked no more
Here, take my loin cloth
This new way is
Whiteman's way
Tear down your sago huts
Here take my steel posts and sheets
This new way is
Whiteman's way
Utter not your chants and spells
Here, take my bible
This new way is
Whiteman's way
Be little no more

Here take my white hand
It's this new way
The Whiteman's way

The Fighter
By Lapieh Landu

Dedicated to Kanau Simon
As I sat under my round hut
Whistling away in the silence
The wind blew heavily
The thunder had cried, the rains had neared

Cold and lonely I gazed out
Only to see darkness hover over me
Almost like a blanket
Bringing fear and uncertainty
In the midst of all the obscurity
Was the sound of an animal or a being?
Whose cry screeched higher into the heavens?
And presence shook the earth

ARIKU, ARIKU, ARIKU- vei ina
Was all it could utter?
That alone was enough
His make was all it took

Fear scurried away
Uncertainty disappeared into the mist
Relief was all that remained in me
For he had come

With weapons of hope and faith
So sharp it murdered doubt

Ambiguity and qualm too
He had hoard the day

In a hurry he was gone
Even before my mind could recollect
The mystery he had secret
The reason for all he did

Now still I sit in my round hut
Waiting for the rain, waiting for the thunder
Hoping to see this mortal, saviour and mystery
My heart knew him only as my one fighter.

ARIKU, ARIKU, ARIKU
I imitate, to hear you call out again
So I feel assured and safe
That I know we'll meet again.

*Ariku = brother
*Ve eina = where are you?

Your World
By Mizraiim Lapa

Body of an old rocky rugged hill
That scales the saltiness of fresh water
Strength of a mountain
You balance flesh and weigh it on your teeth
Four-chambered heart,
that house anger and not love
You prison preys in your stomach,
a valley with no ending
Muscles that can entertain woman
Hot breath that shows concern
Red looks that provide protectiveness

Your body moves in a snake- like fashion,
curse of the serpent has fallen on you too
So dirty and damn attractive to your world
You slip down muddy river banks
destructing the silence of nature
You make me feel like living in your world

Identity
By Mizraiim Lapa

Under the canopy of science
Glass of nature reflect your kingdom, animalia
Class in the lake schooled you to be a reptilian
Flash of lightening photographing you
Flesh in trills of delights
You splashed to your family, the crododyloidea
Bathing in the salt water
The sun soaped you with stares of hot heat
Exposing genes of crocodyloidea
From your super family
You have been ordained
By the law of Your Creator
To be in the order Crocodylia

New Eden
By Martyn Namorong

In the beginning was the Word
And He flew like Paradise Bird
Through floral forests of New Eden
And gave to us this precious land
Did He breathe the Bismarck Breeze?

Into Adams wide nostrils
Did He carve the Great Sepik?
When He ruled from Wilhelm's peak
In land of Gold that floats on Oil
He pitched His tent into the soil
And gave to Abel sugar cane
Much to Cain's great disdain
Did wise Solomon sail this sea?
Did Christ's tears flow the Fly?
Papua New Guinea
Praise the name of God on High

The Lost Melanesians
By Martyn Namorong

YOU have a name for folks like me
Coconuts!
Black on the outside and white inside
Yeah sure I know my people
And maybe I speak their language
But I am not one of them

YOU TOK mi Mangi Mosbi
Boi bilong bikpela siti
Na yu tokim mi olsem
Paps blo yu lusim peles longtaim
So nau yu nogat giraun

Shameful! aint it?
Yeah mate its bloody shameful!
And I cover up my shame
By calling YOU ples tingting
Nogat save bilong yu
YOU're hurt and I'm hurting

Siti boi ino save lo bunara
Na peles mangi ino save lo laptop
Teach me to be me
But do not be like me
I admire you mangi blo ples
YOU are my missing ME

I'm just a cargo boi to Kongkongs
Na yu em papa bilong graun
Het bilong mi go longlong
Na mi salim graun bilong yu
Yeah I sold it for 99 years bro
Sold my soul and sold you off

Everyday
By Gelab Piak

Every day when the sun rises,
My heart aches just a bit more,
Every setting sun quenches the thirst of my hopes.

Every full moon that rises in the dark,
carry my prayers up there until morning
and every time it sinks it takes me down with it.

For I have no life

I wither away with the passing wind that sweeps
And my life is but a lie
A fake just to help me endure the pain I feel within

Every time the sky is not so blue
dark clouds of hatred linger everywhere
and every now and then a thunder storm rages through me.

Every night I sit and stare into my life
it is like dark black water in a well
and I wish, and wish, for all this unending to end.....

But the rains that fall wash away my cries
sometimes my head feels like exploding
but I go to sleep just once more,
and wake once more to another day of the same.

The Dream Keeper
By Gelab Piak

The dream keeper takes away your dreams,
And locks them far away in his dream box,
From then you shall never dream dreams again,
But living in his dreams you shall be.

The streets of gold paint pavements yellow,
The eye of the man sees narrow also,
But behold His justice is a four-edged sword,
It burns a yellow, hollow golden reddish tip,

The dream keeper makes all dreams go away,
Your childhood dreams he makes disappear,
The keeps your dreams in his colourless box,
Where dreams go in and their colours fade,

An evil witch cursed his dreams into the darkness,
So the dream keeper set out to steal every one's dreams,
He takes their dreams and lives in them,
So only the wishing star can wish back his dream,

Come Away
By Ignatius Piakal

There is no promise of fast cars, bikes and blings,
but of buses, Dynas and dugouts.
There is no promise of hotels, motels and cocktails,
but regales of tales and gales of laughter.
Amidst the chit-chat chatter,
of chirrups and chirps,
over gurgles and babbles
of eddies down dales and vales.
Buai stains, black earth and blue skies.
From golden yawns of tired days
to quite cool of a million stars,
Chandelier to a million lives,
witness the passion of this fire
burn beyond the dying embers,
unquenched of eyes aflame,
as I catch the glint in 'em.

Heart beats and head rush,
like the distant roar endless,
of the Baiyer wild in perpetual rush,
beneath ancient Mul of stoic calm,
who thru tufts soft as shifting shapes,
in silent whispers of hallowed zephyrs,
breath your name in the quite cool.
Come away, come away

Dances with Folly
By Ignatius Piakal

How dare you revel in this folly?
Against the wholly,
The holy logic of reason.

How can something so wrong
As a thorn in a thong,
Feel so damn right?

How can I still sow?
When I already know
What bitter harvests await?

These eyes they lie.
When truth I try,
I detest in distaste.

Yet truth I scribe
of truth I bribe
for a penchant of bliss

It thrives and lingers
A ring to many fingers
A tumour to cast away

Yea cast far away!
Away from this fray
To the Hades of thoughts

Dare I disclose what this is?
The pieces of a thesis;
A thesis of psycho-anarchy?

Dare I pull her close?
One shot, last dose.
One shot, blood pool.

So eat and be jolly
Dance on in your folly
The last as the end you beckon

A Lover's Response
By Fiona Potane

Days drip
Weeks soak by
Months form a puddle of reminiscence
It's a weary long trip
I think, I sigh
What we share all the cents
Would never price.
My dice
of omnipotent love.
Either way I shove
Always adds up to You.
The best beau.

From the very start
You stole my heart.
I'm lost, longing, wondering how?
My brain whispers, "Wow"
You took it
Bit by bit
Now you have it all
You make me crawl
Slowly, surely to your realm.

Each dripping day
I pray
An approaching week
To soak into a leak
And then, a puddle
Of bonding to commence.
Then surely I will cuddle
In your arms to prominence.
To that vast unknown future
Us, I will nurture.

Forever and always
It's a maze
But my love lingers on
For every new dawn
With you
Is a love so true.

My Sun
By Fiona Potane

You are my Sun
The shiny, sparkly centre
Of my solar system.
Each dawn I wake
To the beautiful beams of
Warmth and affection you shake
Off that blanky of mine.

As I go off to school
Your round face radiates rays of love.
When you're not with me
My heart is cold, I don't feel your warmth
You're clouded off
By strange satellites:

'friends' I call them.
Yet at the worst of times
When I'm drenched with pain and misery
You brighten my sky.
Your warmth brings me to life.

It's not on your consent
But, if you were absent
Not part of my life
It would be a strife.
A chaotic cluster of planets
Caught in numerous nets;
Of emotions—loveless
Without your charming caress.
Your presence
In essence
Is my entire existence.

You keep me in orbit
My life in rotation
I'll always revolve around
Your field of love.
You're my stunning sun
My hot hearth of health
And my beautiful beam of love.

You are the best
Today is your day to fest
For being a marvellous mother
Like you
There is no other
And its true!

Mom, I love you

The Sea was the Love of my Life
By Reginald Renagi

A long time ago
For those before me,
Life began over the water
Since time immemorial, the sea was there

The sea gave us birth
So too it watched my birth
The sea became my life since then
This love of sea grew over the years

Like a woman's charm, sea seduces all
Loving many ways she nurtures me daily
This love for the sea is a strong bond
For years, we were happy as one

But her obsession found me a new love
Mine mistress turned bride to wife
Life was blissfully happy as any could be
For a while the allure of the sea was forgotten

Pity this love would not share my old love
Alas, happiness was not to last forever
For my love did not understand
To make me choose over love of the sea

The love at home forbade me to go to sea
The love of my youth, she would not understand
My happiness became a ship caught in a storm
For me the pull of the sea was forever strong

The sea became a lifetime journey of adventure
But years makes man wish for a settled life
Forever enchanting the sea seduces all
Leaving home for foreign shores

Since time began, sea made trade and commerce
Her playground was the battlefields of wars
Of supremacy it broke, built and made great nations
Reshaping new business alliances and treaties

The sea gave life for my people
Forever strong is the pull of the sea
Try as I may it keeps coming after me
Yes, before me she was my first love
The sea will always be the love of my life.

The Ship of State
By Reginald Renagi

The high seas of nationhood
A long voyage for a proud ship of state
Master, crew and passengers aboard
The great ship launched with much fanfare
Attended by Royalty with honours bestowed

Every year the story is told many times
Happy are shipowners and shareholders
Master and crew with much to learn
Of a new business, of governance and development
Sailing over the horizon to trade in distant lands

This new ship of state sails the high seas
To markets, business and new relations
With much goodwill and strong alliances

The years told of many good adventures
Distant ports with prosperity and new growth

With each passing of time come new gains
New crew join but always the master remains
With time the master gets good at his trade
In stormy weather, the grip on his helm is sturdy
Less steerage be lost in the stormy seas
High seas and ports, the country pays its way forward

A voyage is a life-long journey for the ship
And the old master also grows weary with age
Each voyage invokes many sad lamentations
Of days of good crews and happy passengers
Now sadly those days are gone forever

Now the master dreams of his younger days
Those good days of honour, trust and responsibility
Now the shipowners and shareholders demand
A young master and a good crew for new stormy seas
New master, sturdy crew and good order has come
And a new ship of state for a new young generation

The Ballad of Bougainville Soldiering By Leonard Fong Roka

The trigger man. The trigger man. The invading trigger man!
He disembarks tough and fierce…
The OC barks orders
He knows, it's time for the jungles.
The shrubs brush his face welcome
He set booby traps and roadblocks
Along suitable garden paths
And waits stealthily and eager

For the blood of a black man

For days and seasons he raids…
Eyes directed and re-directed,
By the point of the barrel…
For who there? The Kawa's blood!
As gunships hover high up, and about—
Mortar shelling, rumbling ahead and beside—camouflaged,
He crawls his way through
Sludge and thorns.

Tired of cruel nights, mosquitoes shrill sickening—
Ambushing nothing but wild bites:
Barking and squealing—he
Rampages the village innocence.
Burning to ashes magnificent beds…
Gunning down and bye,
Good looking broad faces.
And raping my womenfolk for him fruitlessness…
Flagging the Sepik Tambaran Haus.

A week in the wildest fields
Crying—tail between his legs—vexed…
But a day off,
He marches intact up and down
The street of my town and life.
O dastard!

A gun in his right, torture and a woman
To his left.
He chats to the penniless blackman: Kawas, you
Trouble men.

Leaving her at morn…
He, to the jungled ridge.

You know brother,
Prolong bombing and blooding bullets,
He cries…as a spirited gunman
Blast in the tangle
Pins him to the ground
He cries and cries, in blood. He cries for mama in New Guinea

Who say she hears? You infidel,
Poor dog!

The Pains of Love
By Bernard Sinai

I found someone to love and to hold
That special one stays close to my heart
Nay the moon fades and sun grows cold
She will still be that rhythm in my heart

But my fondness for the fruit of the vine
Has made me hurt that one close to my heart
And outside she acts like all is fine
But inside she is I know she is torn apart

What can I do to make it up, my love?
What do I do to make you forgive me?
What can I do to make you whole again?
What can I say to make it right?
My heart yearns to be near you
Absence from you makes my heartache
But I bring pain every time I'm near you
So I will keep my distance for love sake

Books and Beer
By Bernard Sinai

Books and beers, hear em' cheer
For em' say beer make em' head clear
Give em' more dough, mama dear
Em' wantem buy more beer
Very soon me hear em' stutter
Em wantem m-more w-w-w-ine
But em' m-mekem s-s-s-wine noise
T'sol em' just fruit blong vine
Nau mama no givem em' dough
Em go long papa long borrow
But no money, papa say
All for your school I pay
But still em' wantem more beer
Nau em' cheer turn to growl
En very soon em' join in street brawl
All because em' mixem books and beer
Nau em sindaun long jail na luk sori
Inside long bel blong papa mama tu i wari
School ino finish good but em stap long jail
Na nogat money long payem bail
Nau em sindaun na look outside long jail window
Goodpela tingting i come long em
Freedom stap outside long window
Em coverem face blong em in shame
Why na me mixem books and beer!?

Singsing
By Imelda Yabara

Tapa, Pandanas, Mud masks and Spears,
Mud, Paint, Sea shells and Buai,

Heads held high they stride,
They dance side by side,

Plumes on their heads fly high,
Pride shining in their eyes

Drums, Garamuts, kundus,
boom, thump and thud through the night,

Calling all to come and witness the sight,
As Papua New Guinean youths in traditional attire,

Declare Tumbuna style,
"We are ready, this is our time"

Home Coming
By Imelda Yabara

The sea breeze whispers as it sweeps by,
The sun tiptoes across the skyline,
Orange streaks shoot out across the sky,
The sea slaps on the beach as if to say "hi",
Coconut leaves rustle greetings as I walk by,

A red-stained smile makes my heart jump in reply,
Tears run down rheumy eyes,
"You came," he whispers in this beautiful language of mine,

Wonderful shaky old calloused hands reach out,
They hold my hands and trace nose, mouth and eyes,

The scent of sea, wood smoke and freshly cut wood swirl together deliciously,
All around birds, children, insects and people speak,
No jarring noise just blending perfectly,
Sago thatched roofs bring back memories,
Black Palm walls achingly familiar,

White coral scrunches as I sit,
Small, hard leathery palms touch and squeeze my feet,
And wipe away my tears,
As she whispers softly,
"I knew you would come back to me."

ESSAYS

Education: Oppression Before Enslavement
By Corney K Alone

As a patriotic Papua New Guinean, I am saddened by what I read and continue to read about outcome-based education (OBE).

English teachers of secondary schools in Morobe province say the level of written and spoken English is dropping and blame the OBE curriculum for the demise, saying it should be done away with.

People need to understand the appalling situation, honestly debate it and act accordingly – and quickly. The OBE story is heartbreaking, alarming and a serious cause for concern. Look at it this way. Give a select group of students a decent education for 15 years and you will produce intelligent and potential leaders for industry and government.

Now, give another group of students crap education for 15 years and you will produce mediocre and poor leaders. PNG introduced OBE 15 years ago. Soon we expect to see the mass production of a mediocre and poorly skilled workforce.

Hear what the teachers are saying. They do not know where the English curriculum starts or ends. Students are thrown in at the deep end. Previously they were taught spelling, vocabulary, grammar and writing, but not with the new curriculum.

This is a travesty. We cannot allow our children to be poisoned and dumped like this. The quality of education has been sacrificed – resulting in ruined lives. This is flawed national policy, planning, and strategy. St Joseph's College in Port Moresby aptly described OBE as DOA (Dead On Arrival) during a recent inter-school debate. It was spot on.

Let's not kid ourselves. PNG is blindly following a path engineered by foreign consultants that will lead to death in knowledge and skills. Our education system has been hijacked and remotely controlled by so-called donors.

The truth is being ignored by the Secretary of Education and his camp of education planners and strategists in Waigani. The time has come for the parents, guardians and concerned Papua New Guineans to reject the OBE curriculum before we end up with a huge pool of ill-educated people in this country. It is a disaster that is about to happen.

This doctored 'Oppression Before Enslavement' tactic has no relevance and place in my beautiful PNG – abolish it now.

PNG'S Education System – Reform and Neglect

By Bapa Bomoteng

The policy makers write, launch, and celebrate new policies every few years. But what is the yardstick to measure the effects of education reform, and especially Outcome-Based Education since its inception?

We can proudly count our achievements. We have seen the growth of PNG professionals across the board - nurses, teachers, accountants, economists, writers, doctors, judges, pilots, bankers. Over 35 years we have produced university graduates at the highest level and have provided professors to some of the world's leading universities. We have made millionaire entrepreneurs and have many professionals serving overseas. We have come of age.

But today's leaders are products of the old education system of the pre-reform days. What has the post-colonial system contributed to the current workforce and the leaders of the nation?

What was wrong with the old basic Science, Mathematics, Biology, Chemistry, Social Studies, English, Manual Arts and Home Economics that produced the leaders of today? PNG labour is marketable in many parts of the world. This is the result of the old schools. What went wrong with the education reforms introduced in the late 90s and 2000s?

Recently, an Australian government-sponsored university review committee, with Sir Rabbie Namaliu as a member, did an injustice in producing a report undermining PNG's higher education system by not giving a realistic picture of the status of universities. Some parts of the report even denied existence of a couple of schools and courses offered at the University of Technology.

Over the years, education reform architects seem to have tried to systematically kill off the brains of this nation by suggesting the system was not producing results. A government policy some years ago gave lower budget priority to higher education and the result is dilapidated infrastructure in the nation's higher learning institutions. Only recently has the higher education sector received additional funding in science, technology, research and some infrastructure rehabilitation.

The imbalance in funding and lack of training at technical and university levels has left an excess of school leavers and fewer qualified professionals. The system seems to have created more followers and fewer leaders.

With the introduction of OBE and the education reform, all paid for by Australian taxes, the government appears to have produced illiterate elementary to secondary school drop outs, made fit only to return to village life and engage in traditional agriculture. Papua New Guineans are returning to the village and can no longer speak English. No wonder they feel disadvantaged and marginalised.

Those in urban centres whose parents can afford for them to be educated in private schools, or even Australia, get to go on with their education while the others are left to fend for themselves. The gap continues to widen between the haves and the have nots, rural and urban, private and government schools, domestic and overseas scholars.

Where is PNG heading with its education system? Why are we so gullibly accepting OBE or for that matter and any other reform? Reform from what? And for whose benefit?

OBE is one of the killer diseases in PNG's education system. There may be a systematic donor-sponsored illiteracy mindset being forced onto our people. OBE policy will forever change the scenario of high school education after 2010. The results will be known in 2012, when applications are processed for university entry.

Rural elementary students, taught in vernacular languages in their first three years, get spelling, speaking and writing mixed up when they move to Grades 3-8 because of the vernacular and *Tok Pisin* training in their formative years. They are not properly prepared for the basics in English reading and writing skills in primary school. Since we want everyone to enter high school, the system automatically puts all good and bad apples through the process. So far the OBE process has not brought out the best in our students.

I hear of teachers being forced to be "a jack of all trades" in their classrooms. Teachers teach everything in all subject areas with little in-depth knowledge in any subject. More and more parents are sending their children to private schools as they realise the standards are dropping or being compromised by lack of commitment by teachers in the public schools.

Where are we heading with the education reform agenda? Where are we going with OBE? Do the consultants and Waigani experts who have pushed this system, known to have failed in other countries, have some hidden agenda? Why did we change in the first place? Did the old system fail or collapse? Whose music are we dancing to here?

This generation of educators must be held responsible for the rise or the fall of our next generation of Papua New Guineans and the nation's future.

Thirty-Five Years On: Celebrate and Question
By Effrey Dademo

The red, black and gold, with a touch of the bird of paradise flew for the first time on Independence Hill, Port Moresby on 16 September 1975. I was six months old, and had no idea of what had just happened!

PNG last month celebrated 35 years of Nationhood. Reflections of how we've fared as a nation are the order of discussion and I ask a question shared by many in my generation – a new generation of leaders, entrepreneurs, professionals and citizens, of this beautiful country.

Are we Independent, in the true sense of the word?

Exactly five years before 16 September 1975, 16 Papua New Guinean members of the then House of Assembly developed a vision for a new nation.

The Constitutional Planning Committee (CPC) tabled certain underlying principles as the basis for the development of the National Goals and Directive Principles in our Constitution.

These principles were nation building, development of people, participation and decentralisation, consultation and consensus, rights and freedoms, and quality of leadership.

It was from these principles that the vision of PNG was born. It was a vision to ensure human development, equality and participation, national sovereignty and self reliance, wise use of natural resources, and all these through the use of Papua New Guinean ways with the aim of achieving a free and just society.

On the eve of self-government, the CPC declared: "Our Constitution should look towards the future and act as an accelerator in the process of development. It should be related to the national goals that we leaders of this country are enunciating.

"A clear definition of PNG's most fundamental national goals ... is of great importance to the welfare of our people and to the effectiveness of the Constitution in promoting it..."

It is interesting to note that the very first goal of our Constitution was for integral human development, a process described as freeing oneself from every form of domination or oppression to have the opportunity to develop as a whole person in relationship with others.

When I ponder on this goal, it seems obvious that the CPC intended people to be the focus of development of the nation. Have we freed ourselves from all forms of domination and discrimination? Have we adequately recognised and put in place statutory mechanisms to uphold the basic social rights of every citizen?

After 35 years of independence, PNG still faces significant development challenges. There is evidence of extreme hardship facing households. Our living standards are on the decline. The rural population remains at a disadvantage. There are insufficient employment opportunities accorded to our youth. There is worsening law and order. And disturbing health issues reflected in the rise of HIV/AIDS.

There is no shortage of statistics. Our country is ranked 148 out of 175 countries on the UN Human Development Index. Life expectancy for an average Papua New Guinean ranges from 50-60 in rural and urban areas respectively. About 30% of people over the age of 15 do not have cash earning ability, and between 33 and 40 infants die each day from diseases that could be prevented. We have managed to educate only half our women over age 15. Half our population does not have access to clean drinking water and we battle with HIV/AIDS.

In light of these challenges, I have to ask whether we give our men and women equal opportunity to develop, participate and benefit from the development of PNG. Has there been an equalisation of services across the country or are the benefits from project-rich provinces concentrated such that only a portion of the population benefits from the income generated?

Article 25 of the Convention on Civil and Political Rights promotes the right to participate in public affairs. A rights-based approach should be a means to development. Are all citizens in this country able to equally participate in political, economic, social and religious activities?

Do we recognise and respect the rights of every citizen to have equal excess to legal processes and all services both governmental and non-governmental that each citizen requires fulfilling his or her needs and aspirations? In consideration of any matter affecting citizens and their communities, is every citizen of this country able to participate in ensuring their voices are heard?

When our forefathers declared our third national goal to be that of national sovereignty and self-reliance, I am pretty sure they foresaw the difficulties that the cash economy would bring such as poverty, social disorientation, environmental degradation and disturbance of Papua New Guinean or Melanesian ways.

Our challenge has been to blend traditional PNG ways with modernity. It hasn't been easy. Our land has been at the centre of controversy, with differing views of development. Should communal ownership be forgone in favour of individual title? What impact would that have on the communities that depend on their land for their livelihood?

One thing is for certain; we have failed to adopt a bottom-up, participatory planning approach, involving the very people whose interests we should be serving? Is there truly national sovereignty in planning and decision-making?

Self-Reliance is declared to be a means to an end in National Goal 3. Have we been self-reliant in pursuing, negotiating and developing our resource projects, or are we too dependent on foreign advice especially of multi-national corporations?

Our environmental sustainability record is one of the worst in the world despite our having the best laws in the world. With logging concessions in operation without a proper national forest inventory and national forest plan, we don't even fall close to achieving the International Tropical Timber Organisation's sustainable yield definitions and targets.

The focus of the CPC was that our natural resources be wisely used for present and future generations of this nation. How can we plan how much to take out and how much to save, when we don't have proper stocktaking and planning?

What are our "Papua New Guinean ways", and have we tried to achieve development primarily through the use of our own social political and economic institutions?

This is the ideal moment in history to apply the brakes. We should ask ourselves whether the spirit of our Constitution and its goals and directive principles, has indeed been our guardian angel. As a resource rich country, have we achieved true economic independence? Are our gold, copper and oil processed onshore? Is the cost of petroleum products in this country reflective of an oil-producing nation?

This country is so rich in resources that, in the words of one senior statesman, we are an "island of gold floating on a sea of oil".

Our institutions of government, education, commerce, and religion, and most importantly our attitudes, need a complete re-orientation in order that they respond to the needs and aspirations of citizens of this country.

While we celebrate and feel a sense of pride today - an island nation, rich and diverse in cultures, with unique traditional systems - I call on every professional young man and woman to join me in asking these questions. As my daughter turns two today, Independence Day, I also ask these questions on behalf of her generation.

Martin Luther King so famously stated: "I have a dream that one day this nation will rise up and live out the true meaning of its creed…" Although, he was referring to the Emancipation Proclamation signed to end slavery, we also this day, in this nation, have an obligation to ourselves and our children and their children to put an end to a certain "form of slavery".

We have to free ourselves from oppression and suppression! We have been slaves to ignorance, greed, self-centredness, cynicism, complacency, corruption and tyranny. Let's stand up and acknowledge that today we dream, that today this nation will rise up and give meaning to its national goals and directive principles. That tomorrow, we the people of this land will take charge of our destiny. Only then, will there be true Independence!

Still Waiting for the Government to Govern
By Jeffrey Febi

I returned from home bewildered and of course angry, at the continuing lack of government infrastructure - the schools, aid-posts, roads.

I had walked for two days to catch a PMV to travel to Goroka to catch my flight to Port Moresby. My home village is located in a not so remote part of the Eastern Highlands. It shares borders with Wabo (Gulf), and Nomane (Simbu). It used to be okay 12 years ago, the last time I went home.

There are 20 villages in the area I come from. They have a population of between 8,000 and 9,000. Only two primary schools service them, and these are small schools which cannot accommodate more than 200 students in any one year. Teachers from other areas do not want to work here, so a couple of local teachers are doing their best by taking more than one class.

I witnessed the ruins of many aid posts: some totally covered by kau-grass while others continue to stand as if to hold their heads above the surrounding suffocating grasses and shrubs. The existing aid-posts, and the only health centre, are without drugs and short of staff.

The road is overgrown by grass and bush. Small trees grow in the road. Fences have been erected across the road, as no vehicle has driven there for a while. It won't be long before food gardens are planted on the road.

This has been the norm for almost a decade. And no respite in sight. The people who will miss going to school and the people who will die from treatable diseases - who will they blame?

The PNG government has on many occasions boasted about sustained economic growth and increased revenue collections.

So why are these people still suffering? When will they stop carrying coffee bags for days on end only to be robbed by money-hungry roadside coffee buyers who buy beans at much lower prices? Who will hear their cries for much needed basic medical supplies?

I can proudly proclaim that most of the organic coffee beans from unfortunate farmers end up in most of the brands of the popular Goroka

Coffee many people enjoy the world over. Think about it.

We Are Being Overwhelmed by Corruption By Jeffrey Febi

I have seen the best minds I met at university destroyed by corruption. I smell corruption in the breath of those I share buai (betel nut) with on the streets. And I sense the lurking presence of corruption hovering in my dreams.

In the public service machinery, the huge formless and shapeless sculpture of corruption casts a dark shadow over PNG.

State corporations embrace corruption in its most deceptive forms. Many individuals brag openly about their adventures of theft and con deals involving government departments. Pastors and church elders, overwhelmed by corruption's mystique, have opted to trade their sanity for its charms. Even womenfolk give their hearts to this madness.

Many make a decent living from it and think and talk about it almost every day – it is their way of life, it is their culture. The same people joyously ridicule those who do not steal to live decent lives and call them names such as pipia or rabis (rubbish).

Corruption's unhindered growth, and consequent incorporation into our way of life, mocks our Melanesian culture we are so proud of. It effortlessly strolls along our streets, enters homes and kitchens and bedrooms; clothes and feeds innocent children; and pays school fees, compensation, bride price and for guns used in tribal fights and other evil deeds.

I cannot see a hill or a valley not covered by its darkening cloud. It is difficult to see clearly! It is hard to breathe easily. We languish in the shadow of corruption while we turn and twist restlessly in its filth.

Is there still any place untouched by it? How many are out there, who have not yet caught its fever? Who can redeem us? Tell me, any brave one! Sing out loud before hope is lost.

Corruption is entrenched in our way of life. It appears many generations must pass before its suffocating tentacles are burnt to ashes in the bonfires of PNG's faithful sons and daughters.

A Tribute to a Legend and his Legacy
By Sharlene Kylie Gawi

The 9th of April 1936 saw the birth of a leader who would steer a vast and richly diverse nation onto independence. A leader who Papua New Guineans all over this nation loathe and love simultaneously, but respect unanimously.

A leader who has been constantly and consistently involved in the political life of our country from day one.

This legend, born Michael Thomas Somare to Ludwig and Kambe Somare and known today as Grand Chief Sir Michael Somare, celebrates 43 years in PNG politics this year having been first elected into the House of Assembly in 1968.

The front page of the Post Courier on Wednesday the 29th of June read "Family Retires Chief". Jonathan Tannos of the Post Courier reported that Prime Minister of Papua New Guinea, Sir Michael Somare, has been effectively retired from office by his hugely concerned family because he could not coherently make that decision.

Papua New Guineans re-acted in various ways to this reported announcement made by Arthur Somare.

Among the political community there was immediate speculation as to who would take over as Prime Minister of Papua New Guinea. Acting Prime Minister Sam Abal, upon hearing this announcement described this decision by the Somare family as the "ending of a great and historic chapter" of PNG politics.

The National Newspaper, on Wednesday the 29th of June 2011, devoted 4 pages as a Tribute to Retired Prime Minister Sir Michael Thomas Somare. This 4-page spread detailed aspects of his personal life, snap shots of historical moments in his political career and a column applauding "Lady Veronica, the woman behind Sir Michael."

Immortalized on our fifty kina note, Sir Michael Somare set sail on his political career and took the whole country with him as we embarked on a journey to Independence, a journey that began in 1975.

Officially, we marked the occasion and celebrated independence on the 16th of September 1975, realistically, however, independence has been a journey, and continues to challenge us as Papua New Guineans.

Officiating at the main Independence ceremony held in Port Moresby were His Royal Highness Prince Charles, Prince of Wales (representing Queen Elizabeth II); Sir John Kerr, Governor-General of Australia; Australian Prime Minister, Gough Whitlam; and Chief Minister of Papua New Guinea, Michael Somare.

As we celebrate 36 years of Independence this year, or better yet, 36 years of the journey, we also celebrate 43 years of a devoted captain.

A captain who rose to the challenge of steering one of the most diverse nations of people in the world on their journey to independence and self-realization. A captain with a vision and a love for his country and his people.

I salute you Sir Michael, Papua New Guinea salutes you.

For many are called but few are chosen. Indeed many were called, but you were chosen. We applaud you for your leadership and a job well done.

Chinese Threat May Be PNG's Opportunity By Francis Hualupmomi

It appears that the peaceful rise of China has been miscalculated in some parts of the world as a potential threat to the international system.

In reality China is just another ordinary state making waves to restore her lost pride after being humiliated and shamed by the West and Imperial Japan in pre-modern times. China has now accepted Western norms and aggressively integrated into a US-led liberal order.

China's peaceful rise to global prominence is a hybrid balance between socialism and capitalism and her national interest is to attain 'Peaceful Great Power' status through economic development without upsetting the rules of the great power game. Her foreign policy is premised on the philosophy of national strength driven by economic power and strong leadership.

The strategy is to project and build soft power diplomacy with more concentration in developing countries to share its wealth and promote a peaceful and harmonious society.

There are three reasons why China is not a threat. First, she is a developing country with huge internal problems to solve; poverty and corruption being the greatest challenges.

Second, geo-strategically China is still no-match for the US as the great power. Although China is rapidly building its strategic capability, it is not necessarily a challenger. It would take more than a decade for China to be a threat. The US, although declining in power, still poses unchallenged capacity and capability as a global leader.

Third, China is a rising regional not a global power. The US is still the great global and regional power. The US has superior maritime capability and Japan and South Korea are US allies, which make it more difficult for China to challenge the status quo. India, Vietnam and Indonesia may also emerge to balance the ledger against China.

In the future, however, China's expansion and influence in developing countries, such as in the Pacific, are a threat to the US sphere of influence and may cause friction, even war. Any miscalculation on Taiwan may lead

China to war.

A neutral diplomacy between the US and China must be reached consensually to avoid future conflicts. China's peaceful rise is an economic advantage for developing countries like PNG. Play the right card to ensure a win-win situation.

Fought by the Young; Regretted by the Old
By Michael Dom

While PNG's situation may not justify 'bloody' warfare, we are at war. We are at war against corruption in government and throughout the public service system, the very architects and mechanisms that should make our state function.

But it is the State versus the People every day. And clearly the other side have no rules of engagement.

Moreover, the people have been divided for far too long into warring factions; tribal politics under the rhetoric of 'unity in diversity'.

This is only aggravated by our own over-insistence with maintaining tribal customs that are not conducive to life in a modern Melanesia.

Wake up! PNG tribal politics is simply not working for us as a united country! Is it not obvious in the breaking up of provinces, the drive for autonomy, the continued ethnic violence, cronyism, the wantok system?

Where is the development at the grassroots? How can we all be compensated when we have 800+ tribes to satisfy?

There is a rising tide of resentment stirring among working class people; the commonfolk.

We see our youth, our villagers, our struggling farmers, lay workers and street kids being fooled time and time again to support bogus political candidates with faulty party lines.

To be sure, even the so called educated elite of the universities and professionals fall prey to the insidious tactics of some of these 'bigmen'.

We received our independence while the greater majority of our country was still 'living in the stone age'. That is not so today. Let's turn that first mistake on its head.

People, need to start talking to each other. In our work places, in our schools, our homes, churches and communities. With colleagues, neighbours, friends and family.

Start talking about it now. Decide what our communities need. What we aspire to, what we believe in.

In my opinion, we need a revolution. A Melanesian revolution. One of thought and conscience. A revolution that enables our pasin (culture) to shine like a beacon into the darkness that overshadows our development.

A revolution that enables us to transcend the lingering bondage of archaic customs that limits our becoming. A revolution that enables us to transpose our Melanesian principals to be more relevant for the times we live in; to write a new song we all can sing with one voice.

Surely our forefathers would be proud of that. They did not have the education, information and technology nor the lifestyles and freedoms that we have today. We are better off, we should try to be better.

We need leaders with the ability and willpower to take up this revolution. More men like Sam Basil. Let them step up to the mark in 2012. If you want to know them, PNG needs to ask - what do we really value?

Or perhaps I'm too much of an idealist.

At War Against a Dysfunctional State
By Michael Dom

While PNG's situation may not justify bloody warfare, we are at war. At war against corruption in government and throughout the public service system, the very architects and mechanisms that should make our state function.

But it is the State versus the People every day. And clearly the State has no rules of engagement. Moreover, the People have been divided for far too long into warring factions; tribal politics under the rhetoric of 'unity in diversity'.

This is aggravated by our own over-insistence in maintaining tribal customs not conducive to life in a modern Melanesia. PNG tribal politics is not working for us as a united country. It is obvious in fragmenting provinces, the drive for autonomy, ethnic violence, cronyism, and the *wantok* system.

Where is the development at the grassroots? How can we all be compensated when we have 850 tribes to satisfy? There is a rising tide of resentment stirring among the commonfolk.

We see our youth, our villagers, our struggling farmers, lay workers and street kids being fooled time and time again. Even the so-called educated elite falls prey to the insidious tactics of some of these *bigmen*.

People, need to start talking to each other. In work places, in schools, homes, churches and communities. With colleagues, neighbours, friends and family. Start talking now. Decide what our communities need. What we aspire to, what we believe.

We need a revolution. A Melanesian revolution. One of thought and conscience. A revolution that enables our *pasin* to shine like a beacon into the darkness.

A revolution that enables us to transcend the lingering bondage of archaic custom that limits our becoming. A revolution that enables us to transpose our Melanesian principals to be more relevant for the times we live in; to write a new song we all can sing with one voice. Surely our forefathers would be proud of that.

We need leaders with the ability and willpower to take up this revolution. Let them step up to the mark. PNG needs to ask - what do we really value?

A Day in the Life of Awi Magret in Sol Nomane
By Mathias Kin

On a Wednesday in early November 2009, I hitched a ride on Uncle Ben's Land Cruiser for Deri village, 50 kilometres south of Kundiawa Town in Sol Nomane. I had been invited to attend a marriage party. It was raining as we hit the dirt road at Munuma so I was apprehensive of the newly graded South Simbu roads as we traversed the ever winding bends towards Gumine and further onto Sol Nomane. However Uncle Ben's machine was truly trustworthy - the Japanese made these vehicles for the rural roads of Simbu!

The next day Thursday afternoon, I went down to Deboma. There I sat at the edge of the cliff enjoying the spectacular Wahgi gorge painted beautifully gold by the setting sun over the Digine Mountains. Beyond the cliff far below me, the canopy of willow trees, their leaves flipped over white simultaneously by the down flowing convectional currents from higher slopes and further at the bottom of the canyon, the spectacular crashes of the mighty Wahgi against the ancient black Maril Shale, all presented a totally different setting to the Waigani polished shoes and neck tie scenes among whom I had roamed in mid-2009.

Suddenly from the corner of my eyes I saw two figures slowly but surely walking up this threadlike steep track with ease and competence, each carrying huge loads on their backs. It was Awi Magret and her daughter Mary. It then struck me that in this twenty first century our mothers are still performing unbelievably very gruelling jobs, chores only fit for mules. So I decided to do this story; "*a day in the life Awi Magret in Sol Nomane.*" I wanted the world to know the story of Magret and her people in this part of Papua New Guinea.

Magret is about 60 years old and Mary in her late twenties. They are each carrying several bundles of *kunai* grass and had been climbing up from the thin alluvial flats below at Pleme where for centuries tons of soil and organic matter had been deposited by the mighty Wahgi as it snaked its way carrying most of its contents to the useless swamps of the Papuan Gulf. These bundles of grass tied together and strapped onto the head and suspended on the back are about 30 kilograms each. Twenty similar loads will be thatched together to roof their new in-law's house.

The next day Friday 13th was a blue windless morning. There was excitement buzzing through the village of the marriage. Magret's grandson Hauba will be married to Priscila from Bosila village, two kilometres away. Today Magret looked cool in her coloured *meri blaus* and matching *laplap*. When I imagined the previous day's encounter, she did not show any sign of it. Yesterday had simply been another day in her life.

We arrived at Bosila to a huge welcome of war cries and *singsings*. There were over three hundred people here today. Five huge pigs were slaughtered and cooked in a pit oven. There was so much food for everyone. It is an occasion where new friendships are fostered and old ones rekindled and enriched. It is also an opportunity where the "*bigman*" make long eloquent speeches to enhance his status. The last ritual is the eating of the pig lard by the new couple which legalizes the marriage. The events of today had been a grand show of Simbus' rich culture. By 5.00 pm, we came home with our new family member.

Deri village is home to 400 hardy Simbu people and is one of hundreds of villages in South Simbu. These villages are located at 1500 to 2000 meters high and have pleasant spring climates. From here, one can take breathtaking views of many areas of central highlands. The people domesticate pigs and grow *kaukau* and many other food types in huge gardens. They participate in the formal cash economy only during the coffee season. In this year's harvest, Magret's family will use their coffee money to reciprocate the recent party. She will use the remaining money on other traditional obligations.

This is a beautiful story of a perpetual uncomplicated existence.

On the bigger picture, PNG is 35 years old and has six million people. Our country earns billions each year from our minerals, hydrocarbons and cash crops. Our people are educated in many disciplines and thousands more graduate every year. Our modern communication and transport systems had ensured our world is smaller than it was a few years back. Even our dominant government can afford a luxury jet to fly them around the globe.

Despite these gains, PNG's social and economic indicators are the worst in the world. Many villages lack basic service. Our people are dying every day from diseases. News of criminal activities frequents the media and the shantytowns of our cities continue to grow as our rural people flock to the cities to access services. While in the corridors of Waigani, our elected representatives and their unelected collaborators and government bureaucrats continue to embezzle government resources without fear. In all truth, our living standard has deteriorated since the Aussies left our shores.

In our feature story, life hasn't changed much for Magret and her family since independence. There are others in our mountains, on the coasts and on the islands that identify well with her. So how do we draw a fitting conclusion to this familiar story? In the last 35 years, our politicians have mismanaged this country so much and left our people in great despair and deceit. How long can it take before we become another Nigeria and Angola, states in Africa who have so much oil and gas, yet its people are the poorest in the world? If our politicians do not change their style of leadership, we are not far off from reaching that dreadful highpoint. Sadly Awi Magret and her kind all over PNG do not know that this great calamity is about to befall them in the very near future.

The Beginnings of Kundiawa Town
By Mathias Kin

Located under the corridor of a 500-meter tall limestone outcrop stretching east to west in the north, Kundiawa town is a bustling town with an estimated population of over 15,000 people. It is the capital of the Simbu province and is home to the best hospital in Papua New Guinea. This story of the beginning of Kundiawa town starts 77 years ago under very unlikely circumstances, a meeting of two leaders from vastly different worlds.

In 1934, Chief Bongere of the Kamaneku tribe had a garden at today's Kundiawa Works Compound. One day, some strange people came from the east and made camp near the garden. They took some corn from the garden and as payment left some shells and an axe covered in the corn leaves in the garden. Very early next morning, these aliens had gone west. Some people who hid in the nearby bushes told Bongere of these strange events.

Many days later these strange people returned. Bongere, being a big fellow and a fight leader for his tribe, confronted them. Before Bongere could do anything silly, these intruders took him to his garden and showed him the items they had hidden there. Bongere was surprised with these strangers' sincerity and was pleased with the instant wealth he had gained for some nothing corn. He promptly became friends with these people, especially their leader William Bergmann. Bergmann told Bongere that he would return soon and build his house to live with him there.

In those days, the present day Kundiawa town area was a fighting zone for the Kamaneku and Endugla tribes and their allies. For this reason, the area was never permanently settled. The Ega area where the school and mission headquarters is today situated was owned by the Kamaneku tribe. The Premier Hill area known as Tema and the Malaria area were owned by the Endugla tribe.

A year earlier the Taylor-Leahy patrol in April 1933 brought the first white men the Simbu people had seen. The Catholic Missionaries led by Fr. Alfonse Schaefer came through the area in November 1933 having crossed the Bismarck Range from Bundi and settled at Mingende. The Lutheran

Missionaries under the leadership of Reverent William Bergmann came through the area from Finchafen through Markham and Goroka in May 1934. That was when they encountered Chief Bongere. As he promised, Reverent Bergmann came back to settle at Ega on the 12th of September 1934.

On that day Bongere came down from his Keakge village on Tokma Mountain with a big white pig and killed it in front of his new friends. He then rubbed *tanget* leaves into the blood of the pig and planted it in the soil. This way, he officially signalled that their land was given to Bergmann and the Lutheran Mission. This was the beginning of a close relationship between Bongere and Bergmann. The locals called Bergmann "Berman" and others called him Kamanekumugl meaning Kamaneku tribesman.

There were two reasons Bongere and his Kamaneku tribesmen easily befriended Bergmann and gave their land to him. Firstly, these aliens would be a physical barrier between the two tribes from further troubles. The people had already seen the power of the white men's fire sticks from the earlier patrols. They believed that by being friendly, these aliens would side with them in the event of an attack from the Enduglas. And secondly, Bongere and his Kamaneku tribesmen did not want these people who owned everything and knew everything good to go to another tribe. They wanted them to be close to them so that they would benefit from all these goodness. Chief Bongere's astuteness served its purpose - today the two tribes have not seen any tribal fights since then and their sons and daughters are educated well-to-do personalities all over PNG and abroad.

The Mission quickly built an airstrip which today is the Simbu Airport and the first plane landed on the strip a month later. In the ensuing months and years the station was an important stopover for prospectors, missionaries and administration officers passing through from Benabena, Bundi and from the Hagen posts.

In early 1935 after the killing of two Catholic missionaries in the Gembogl Valley, *Kiap* Jim Taylor established the first Chimbu-Whagi post at Tema, now Premier Hill. From here these *kiaps* carried out many punitive expeditions into the Gembogl area to avenge these killings. They killed tens of tribesmen from among the tribes there. Sadly these killings were not recorded and the outside world never knew of these bad acts. Mr Taylor even took away more than 50 tribesmen as prisoners all the way to

Salamaua on the Morobe Coast. Most of them perished and never made it back to their families in Gembogl.

In the 1940s, the Second World War was to have a devastating set back on the positive progress of the church work in the area. Reverent Bergmann and other missionaries of German origin including Father Schafer from Mingende Catholic mission were interned in Australia. During this time, the Ega and the Mingende stations were occupied by the Allied forces. When Bergman returned after the war, his station was left in tatters. Bergmann had to start all over again to rebuild. And soon after, through the hard work of these missionaries and their indigenous workers, the station was brought back quickly to its former state. Ega again became an important centre for the spread of the Lutheran Church throughout Simbu and the highlands.

By 1953 the Highlands Highway was built through the Chimbu-Wahgi post from Goroka. This post, later named Kundiawa, became the capital of Chimbu in July 1966 when the area was declared a district of its own from Eastern Highlands. Kundiawa has today grown to be an important commercial and government centre for the Central highlands.

Had it not been for the shrewdness of Bongere and the inspiration and entrepreneurship of his friend Bergmann, we would not have a Kundiawa like we do today.

How to kill Inferiority Complex
By David Kitchnoge

Until recently, most Papua New Guinean societies were characterised by a patronising culture where questioning the authority has been unheard of. Our big man culture fostered such a deep-seated mentality that no member of the community is bigger than the one individual figurehead. This person, usually the tribal chief, would be law unto himself and anyone who was seen to be not acting in accordance with his rules was made to face drastic consequences and even death.

Such a culture suited our traditional 'enclosed' societies at that time. I use enclosed for want of a better word to describe a social grouping whose political, social and geographical boundaries were relatively limited. Tribal and clan hostilities mostly over geographical territory and land ownership were common occurrences then and so it made sense to organise ourselves in the manner that we did. There was a great need for an individual figurehead, the big man, who was allowed to rule almost like a dictator for the greater good of our individual tribes and clans. Such a system ensured social order prevailed within our little tribal nations at that time.

Then came the intruders with their salt, axe heads, laplaps, firearms and a new belief system. They used these basic yet powerful tools with great effect and slowly went about creating a new layer of social structure within our traditional cultures and imposed themselves right at the top of the power pyramid. They assumed the roles of our social, political and economic powers and also attained recognition and acceptance of their status as the new 'powers' in our social hierarchy. Our awestruck ancestors were too naïve to resist this new social imposition in a similar fashion to the Maoris of New Zealand. But our social structure was and still is quite different to the Maoris in that we are a country of more than 700 different tribes, unlike them, and so we could not put up a united resistance as they did.

So we ended up accepting their ways and allowed them to conveniently substitute themselves as the authority in the new social order. The development of derogatory phrases such as 'yesa masta', 'bos boi', 'kanaka' and so on in the colonial era are symptoms of this rather arrogant imposition. Because of our traditional big man social structure, it is in our subconscious mind to be a submissive people and the white man simply played along this existing cultural reality to impose himself and caused us to submit to him. The acceptance of this new power has sadly remained in our collective national intuition to this day.

And this is where the problem lies for us. I've always believed that the main reason our country has made little progress in the last three decades, despite the large amounts of wealth we've had at our disposal, was because Papua New Guineans were too afraid to speak up, challenge the status quo and offer alternatives to issues. For instance, I work in a professional environment where indigenous Papua New Guineas are too scared to challenge their expatriate colleagues. And if a fellow indigenous person is brave and intelligent enough to do so, they turn around and see him or her in a very negative light and brand him or her a 'big head'. If this isn't self-defeating, then I don't know what is.

My experience so far is that this problem is deeply rooted among Papua New Guineans, and unless we break free from this repression of inferiority complex, we will never ever get anywhere. We should respect people's position and authority but should not be afraid to stand up and hold our own regardless of whether that person is white, black, yellow or coloured. I acknowledge that the 'yesa masta' culture has its roots in the way our traditional big man culture is organised. But times have changed and our social hierarchy has changed substantially. The new big man in the imaginary social structure in our mindsets today is not the same big man of our forefathers. He is not the great warrior that defeated our enemies and protected our tribes to warrant our unequivocal admiration, respect, trust and submission.

So we must move on and move away from this delusion that someone is right simply because he or she has different looks than us and, therefore, appears to us to be the big man.

I have seen great indigenous talents wasting away and not reaching their full potentials because they choose to be meek and submissive. When we go chickening around as individuals, our group, organisation and society misses out on something because we don't get to consider things from a different perspective. We narrow our world view and cause ourselves to be vulnerable to changing circumstances. In other words, our collective innovative abilities are being severely handicapped because we keep on doubting ourselves and are struggling badly to part with inferiority complex.

Don't get me wrong. I am not advocating insubordination. Insubordination is born out of arrogance and it is when someone deliberately chooses to not follow lawful directions although he or she knows it is the right thing to do. There is a fine line between arrogance and self-confidence, and we can be confident without being arrogant. If you think there is a better way of doing something, then bring it up rather than saying 'yesa masta' and simply doing what you are being told to do.

Inferiority complex is ironically being reinforced in our consciousness today through our education system. We are being taught predominantly about the arrival of aliens as 'the' history of our country. And it is not. All our history text books are filled with sketches and photographs of steamships, bearded missionaries and 'discoverers' and their flags and maps.

But where are the stories about our true heritage? Why can we not learn our true history about how our ancestors lived for thousands of years before the aliens arrived? Why can't someone teach us about how good we have always been as architects, builders, agriculturalists and seafarers before the aliens arrived? Why can't someone teach our children about our true identities as Melanesians?

Knowing our true history and how good we have always been will free us of the bondage of inferiority complex and empower us to move forward with confidence. Please stop teaching us this nonsense that some bearded loser came in some fancy vessel all those years ago and 'discovered' us and raised some stupid flag to 'claim' us.

We are a country of indigenous people and we must know our own indigenous history first before learning about how other people illegally intruded into our lives and caused us to unnecessarily submit to them.

Island Home Conversion
By Lapieh Landu

I call home an 'island state'. An island certainly, but also small portion of land surrounded by the multitudes of a beautiful ocean blanket from where the riches of biodiversity are found. My isle as a portion of land within the Pacific Ocean resonates for and with my people. The dimdims sit within their glass and marble enclaves looking beyond their shores to mine for reasons we do not understand. My supposition would be they are reasons of cruel misjudgement, ill reasoning and bitter assumption. Indeed, one could collectively say they are culture judgments.

My people sit within their huts, in their gardens, among their children and debate this judgement. We say to ourselves, we are rich in resources, why do we need to look to others to show us a different way? The light skin people, they arrive on our shores, mistreat us, rob us and pretend to befriend us, what for we ask? To build bridges of trust? Or bridges over the culture and values which our fore fathers laid down for us.

They use this word "development" as if it is a fruitful phrase. What is this word? For it is all very new to us. My people were told that development was needed in my island state. It was explained as a concept; if you allow development you will be recognized.

Why do we need development? To whose standards are we trying to develop ourselves; to the standards of America? What a selfish thought. An egotistical state only interested in establishing a power hungry hegemony.

I really despise this word, hegemony. A word used to describe uniformity to the interests of one's country, meaning that all nations, big or small, poor or rich, capable or incapable, are all expected to measure up to one particular state standard and line of thought.

My rebel of a mind cannot understand what the elders before me had in mind. Did they think that development was some kind of new Christ to save them from their hardships?

I do not blame them for their curiosity and, more recently, the loss of my culture, things I cannot get back. Instead, I blame them for completely letting go of their belief systems, which were my belief systems and my cultural dignity.

I regret to say that I cannot speak my mother tongue, but that of a new wave of dialogue called 'slanguage', which is comprised of Australian English, German Pidgin and the American culture of broken English and street slang, the new thing of my era.

The introduction of slanguage in all aspects is derogatory because it has bastardized my bubus tok ples, my cultural wealth. It has thrown down the drain my cultural heritage and distinctiveness. I stand with shame to reveal that I have lost that part of my tradition.

I now stand in awe at others of my own generation who still have this part in them. It is a rare case to find an 80's kid like me with three languages, English, Pidgin and their own language. I wish I was home grown, and then I wouldn't have this problem.

And just when I thought this was my greatest problem I now face this new one of dealing with the alteration to my island home. My islands around me, beautiful tranquil atolls are now plunging back deep into the seas; animals and species that are striking and rare sliding off the face of the earth, and all the splendour of the rainforests disappearing.

I don't ever want to have to look back at this land and say "This place used to be a stretch of beautiful trees", or "We used to go diving here till the tailings were disposed of . . . ."

The world is not a subjective entity. It is a shared good. There is no reason why my children and their children should not see what I see and enjoy the surroundings that my home has to offer. It is their human right and fulfils their human needs. Where have our long term prospects for humanity gone?

Undeniably my island home has transformed. Although I see a hazy prospect for its abundance and rarity I know we are blessed and thus I have faith in its salvation and the continuation of its future. Island people have heart; island people have brains; island people have souls. It is the utilization of these organs that we lack and have forgotten.

The Political Economy of Everything That's Wrong in Developing PNG
By Martyn Namorong

My name is Martyn Namorong; I was born in Baimuru, Gulf Province. In PNG that doesn't mean I'm from Gulf because my parents are from different provinces. My mum is from Western Province and my Dad is from Madang. I regard myself as being from Western Province because I grew up there- mostly in a remote Rimbunan Hijau (RH) logging camp called Kamusi. I am thus, familiar with the languages, customs and oral histories of my mum's people.

My introduction to the phenomenon of neo-tribalism was at high school here in Port Moresby during the last decade. The key question that arose being, "What does it mean to be a Papua New Guinean?" It is easy to identify a New Irelander, or Sepik or Engan but who is a 'Papua New Guinean'- and the fact of the matter is there isn't any. So every time someone asked me where I was from I simply said PNG although I knew they were inquiring about my home province. Today however, my notion of being from PNG is not as concrete as it used to be.

In 2010 I dropped out of medical school because I had not performed well academically. I was hoping to return this year to university but for reasons unknown to me I haven't been accepted back to repeat Year4 Bach.Med.Surg. While it has been a testing time of my life it has also been a time of huge change in terms of how I perceive myself and the world I live in. I always thought all my life that I was destined to great things and make a difference to humanity. Today, faced with the uncertainty about the future and the hardship of living in the city, I'm more concerned with being able to survive each day. I am more concerned about my own welfare than saving the world.

In talking about my situation I was hoping to give some context to the challenges faced by many other fellow Papua New Guineans. Herein lies the dilemma faced by this nation- what does it mean to be a Papua New Guinean?

The system of education in this country is a failure trap. It is supposed to groom Papua New Guineans but all it does is it produces a lot of failures. In grade 8 ten thousands get thrown out, in grade 10 and 12 thousands more fall through the crack in the system. This is the failure trap. Students spend much of their lives learning about ideas in arts, science and mathematics and are not prepared for both the cash economy and the subsistence economy. I my case, I regret going to medical school because now I am just an unskilled person. I am definitely not skilled to survive in the savannah of East Trans-Fly nor do I have formal qualifications to be recognised in the cash economy. Thus by default I sell betel nut on the street like many other disenfranchised people.

Hundreds of thousands of young people around this nation are trapped like me. For some hopelessness and depression lead to suicide. I lost three of my colleagues from year 12 who committed suicide with-in 2 years of dropping out of year 12. A fellow medical school dropout is now a patient in the psychiatric ward. I believe the mental health of many young people deteriorates once they are caught up in the "education trap". There is an intense feeling of shame associated with loss of self-esteem once someone drops out of school. As for me I tried to deal with my mental state by engaging with my former colleagues at high school and medical school. I figured from the suicides of my year 12 colleagues that what they had done was go into a downward spiral by isolating themselves.

Many try to escape reality by resorting to drugs, alcohol and risky sexual practices. Others take out their frustrations on society through juvenile delinquencies, petty crimes, fights, sexual violence and other indictable offences. I totally empathize with all of them because I now understand what it's like to lose everything including one's dreams and ambitions.

Many who do not understand the psyche of those of us being disenfranchised think we have *'an attitude problem'*. When reduced to the simplest elements there is an *'I don't care about anything or anyone including myself'* attitude amongst most of us. Many males make wrong choices and become a nuisance/threat to society. They don't care if the police or their rivals kill them nor do they have second thoughts about prison. After all once you feel like you've lost everything, what more is there to lose? It is suicidal behaviour. That is why band-aid solutions or knee-jerk reactions such as awareness activities on HIV/AIDS, substance abuse, toughening of laws or promotion of sporting activities have been categorically ineffective in curbing the chaos the PNG.

The antidote to crime in this country is to enable everyone to earn a living so that they are able to meet some of the challenges they face in life and achieve personal goals. Obviously, some challenges are difficult for individuals to handle and individuals with mental health issues need professional help.

In order to bring meaningful and sustainable change in the physical and social settings of this nation one has to liberate its people from the education trap. I'm referring to every Papua New Guinean, may they be in the urban or rural areas. A married man in a village who cannot sustain his family within the subsistence economy will commit crimes to make ends meet. Likewise a man in the urban setting would do something similar. Young women who are unable to participate in either economy are vulnerable to prostitution and suicide. Uncertainty about the future creates negative sentiments thus manifesting in the kind of law and order problems faced by the country.

The solution is not necessarily to 'teach a person how to catch fish' but to give them a net. I believe it's now fair to comment that microfinance institutions in Papua New Guinea have failed in providing people that net. Politicians, Churches, NGOs and business interests have been excellent distributors of free handouts instead of the 'net'. The net I'm referring to is the ability to trade goods and services and/or labour. Our rural people need efficient and affordable transport networks to move goods to local and global markets and to access services. Our urban people need jobs or financial assistance to start small businesses.

Earning an income brings enormous benefits to the individual and their community. People who have money are less of a burden others as well as the state. For example, people with money are able to send their children to private schools and seek healthcare at private hospitals thus easing the pressure of state health and education facilities. People with money are more likely to have access to technology that makes life easier and more productive. A villager with good income can send his children to school and should they fall into the education trap he is able to bail them out by sponsoring them elsewhere or making them partners/employees.

Unfortunately, there is too much hypocrisy and tokenism from all parties involved in aid and development. People want to be seen to be trying to address issues without actually doing anything of substance. That is why news media are full of stories about conferences, symposiums, summits, workshops, forums, etc… where everyone spends huge amounts of money on stipends, venue fees, accommodation of guests, etc… Worse still are donor projects that are handed over to communities only to disintegrate with time. If a classroom is built or a water supply project or are road for that matter, what happens with regard to their long term maintenance? Communities where people don't have income generating opportunities cannot possibly guarantee the sustainability of donor projects.

I believe change is driven by innovation and innovative people are empowered people. When my home village of Malam, in the Morehead LLG area of the Western Province was being built at a new site, it coincided with a period in 1995 where the Commonwealth Scientific Industrial Research Organization (CSIRO) was buying acacia seeds at K80-K100 per Kilo. Many villagers decided to use some of their income to buy corrugated iron sheets for their houses. All villagers had no problems pay school fees and airfares for students to fly to high school. Today Malam people are very proud of their village which has a main street down the centre lined by flowers and trees. Many homes of course have metal roofs and villagers exaggerate that pilots get confused whether they're at a village or government station. Self-generated changes address the needs and aspirations of individuals and communities and are more profound in how they inspire and motivate the people.

Malam is also where a CSIRO project funded by AUSAID flopped. The villages of Malam, Kwiwang and Bensbach were chosen as sites for the distillation of essential oils from two plant species found in the savannah. The projects were doomed from the start. Firstly, no management structure was put in place to manage the project once the donor pulled out. Secondly, markets were inaccessible and there was no distribution network created. There also were various other technical flaws that made the project resource/labour intensive and inefficient. People became disillusioned and gave up production altogether. All production equipment have been dismantled and are rusting away in tall grass. Imposed change can be positive but is usually temporary if individuals and communities aren't empowered to take ownership of the new developments.

I don't believe handouts solve issues other than cover them up for another time. This has been so profoundly manifested in my life such that I now tell people, "I don't need your money; I need an education and a job". Perhaps more irritating for me is that some people think they know what is best for me. While expert advice is valuable, an expert who is not fully versed with the unique circumstances of each case is not in a position to give a fully rounded assessment. The CSIRO are experts in the sciences and failed the villagers in the economics of the project. Likewise a full assessment of a project not only addresses my points but various other issues I may not fully understand.

I don't dream anymore, I am grounded in the reality. I grapple with the facts as they are. Perhaps there are too many visionaries and dreamers such that no one is there to deal with the reality of life in Papua New Guinea. Even a vast majority of people who a trapped like me do not wish to deal with reality. That is why fast money schemes continue to thrive and voters are gullible towards politicians.

Bill Clinton is famous for saying that his number one campaign issue was the economy. In developed countries growth and employment are at the heart of government policies. If we are to become a fairer, wiser, healthier, happier society by 2050 we need to remove impediments' to income earning opportunities for all Papua New Guineans. By addressing the bottlenecks that prevent everyone from meaningful participating in income earning opportunities, we will address issues such as law and order, food security, HIV&AIDS, and etc...

I have deliberately said nothing about what the government should do. All I can say in reference to the government is that it must implement all that it has been planning to do. There are so many well-meaning plans that are gathering dust on the shelves of state agencies. This nation is being governed on an ad hoc basis with decisions being made solely for perpetuating the survival of the ruling class instead of addressing fundamental issues that affect the nation.

I must conclude by thanking Dame Carol for the Informal Sector Act that protects me at my roadside buai market. This is a classic example of giving people the opportunity to be self-sufficient or in my case relatively autonomous. I bought an internet modem that I use to access the internet mainly to publish on my blog and to communicate via email as well as social network sites such as Twitter.

Why PNG Sports Teams are Utterly Hopeless
By Martyn Namorong

"All warfare is based on deception"... Sun Tzu on The Art of War

Every year millions are spent on sporting codes throughout Papua New Guinea. Huge contingents of athletes and teams are sent overseas only to perform poorly. Sports administrators always seem to find excuses to cover up for their failures. Thus, there are no autopsies done to identify weaknesses and put forward strategies to improve performance. No goals or performance indicators are set as a yardstick by which everyone within and without the sporting community is able to evaluate sporting codes.

The pride of Papua New Guinea is also a source of its greatest national shame – The PNG Kumuls. Boy, do they get slaughtered on the field by almost every team they are up against. Rugby league is truly PNG's national sport. Every year or so the entire nation holds it breath as they hope that against all the odds, that the National team may snatch a rare victory. Time after time they are disappointed. (It is ironic therefore that the Kumuls major sponsor is Telikom, whose data and voice services are so bad).

Let me clarify here that this article relates mainly to team sports rather than individual sporting activities. Ryan Pini's gold and Dika Toua's silver medal performances at the Melbourne Commonwealth Games are proud moments in PNG's National History. Francis Kompaon's para-olympic medal from the Beijing Paralympics is also a proud sporting achievement. Team sports on the other hand have had dismal performance records.

Team sports continue to fail due to cronyism and neo-tribalism. They've become family or regional affairs with the recruitment of members from within certain social circles. I must also clarify that I do not refer to cricket and softball because they are sports that have always been traditionally associated with particular regions. The issue of neo-tribalism surfaced recently after the pathetic performance by the Kumuls at the world cup last year with many letters to newspapers which contained prefixes or suffixes to the word Kumul.

Sports administrators do not need to look elsewhere for answers. The sport of Aussie Rules has been doing extremely well recently. The PNG

Mosquitoes and the junior team Binatangs have been stinging their way to victory. AFLPNG has got everything right from Administration to recruitment of talent. Whereas participation in other sporting codes is limited to entry by connections, AFL is more open to the community. Being able to cast a wider net in recruiting talent results in AFLPNG discovering rough diamonds that can then be polished into crowning jewels of the code.

There has to be greater accountability not just in terms of the use of finance rather in providing value for money in sporting outcomes. I'll leave the last word to Sun Tzu "In war, then, let your great object be victory, not lengthy campaigns"

What Independence Means to Our People
By Reginald Renagi

PNG'S Independence is tantamount to the right of every citizen to govern their own house in village, town or city. Independence gives our beautiful country the right to govern itself and to own its destiny.

Independence empowers me as a PNG citizen to interact freely with everyone in my own country and in the world. It also means that, as a citizen of PNG, I can say what I feel and see happening in my country and I can say it without fear or favour.

A lack of independence means that the most important decisions of our country are able to be taken by foreign interests. This is already present in our country, with parliament and government proving their inability to safeguard the people's well-being and welfare for many years now.

Independence is the right of Papua New Guineans to be properly governed under a home-grown constitution which sets the framework for our democracy. Our constitution protects our human rights, language, culture and traditions; and our nationality. Independence means an enjoyment of all things PNG; including fully benefiting from our economic development.

Sovereignty provides our people with power to stimulate national development: agriculture, commerce, industry, immigration, the negotiation of international treaties, expanding markets and promoting foreign relations and investment.

To me, independence means self-government, our own government, ruling ourselves, freedom from all forms of political subjugation, direct control. Not being influenced by any other country.

People agree to be governed so that their rights (life, freedom, happiness) will be safe-guarded. The job of government is to protect the rights of the people. A government is good when it does this. The government must do what the people say, because the people made it. When the government does what the people say, it is democracy.

In PNG, this does not always happen - making the people suffer, despite many changes of government since Independence in 1975. Sometimes the government we have acts badly and not in the national interest. On many occasions it has not protected the rights of the people.

When this happens, the people start to think of a new government, a good government, one that will protect their rights.

Sometimes the people of this country are alienated by the many problems the government has not addressed. Sometimes these people want to make their land into a new country. Many Papua New Guineans have felt this way for many years. It is easy to see why they do not want to be part of the old, bad PNG.

Papua New Guineans must be free to say what they want of their government, and they must be listened to. All people in PNG are equal. God wants every person to have rights. Sometimes bad people in our government try to take away these rights (life, freedom, happiness).

It is smart to change things with much caution. People should not cast off an old government for a silly reason. They should do this only when the government does something very bad.

The people should cast off the government when it tries to take away the rights of the people. There has been a betrayal of PNG for many years by politicians and bureaucrats for apparent personal gain.

These same betrayers were earlier defenders of workers and fighters for the poor. But they have since governed for apparent personal gain and promoted corruption and made our people suffer. These acts of betrayal will eventually destroy PNG.

For the ordinary citizen, Independence Day and its related annual celebrations had little meaning. After 35 years the people are not impressed in any way with a badly governed PNG. Independence celebrations have been reduced to a mere show off for government.

A brief excursion from the inability of the political leadership to suppress crime and violence and improve the quality of life for every man, woman and child in our country.

Many, perhaps most, parts of PNG are in abject poverty and cannot change for the better until the country has fresh, new, visionary leadership and a progressive and transformational government.

We seem not to have the political will today. But we pray for the coming of a new dawn with a new crop of young political leaders who our people hope will save our beloved country for tomorrow's generation. May God bless my country and its people.

"So what is the Story that I should tell?"
By Scott Waide

Tucked away behind the Nobnob mountains on Madang's north coast is a small school – Nobnob Primary School.

Its students are the liveliest bunch of youngsters. Keen to learn and well behaved. Even when the teacher's not there. But like many schools in PNG, the fibro classrooms show the wear and tear of the generations of kids who have passed through.

I was visiting the school to find a good vantage point where I could take some still photographs with Madang town in the far distance. Walking into a classroom, I met a teacher and asked if it was all right if I took a few pictures of the school and the children.

Nobnob Primary doesn't have the luxury of brand new classrooms but it does have a well maintained playing field and a tiny library. I guess, that's what's really important to kids – being able to play and enjoy growing up and being able to learn.

Then you think to yourself: How many of our political leaders would choose to send their children to schools like Nobnob? I can't answer that for you. Some of the children, wide-eyed and curious, clutching worn copies of Oxford dictionaries, stared as I shot off a few stills. I wanted to tell a story. But what story?

I've seen the 'run-down school' story repeated a hundred times. So what new story was I going to tell? A story about children not achieving their dreams because government subsidies aren't paid on time? A story about demoralised teachers struggling with pay and living conditions as the cost of goods continues to rise? A story about teachers trying to decide whether they should have salaries deposited into a bank account, only to have ridiculous fees charged?

My university lecturers would have said, 'Give the story a human face, Scott. Make people see that it's not just about statistics on flashy Powerpoint presentations. The kind that aid donors and government officials love to play with in air conditioned conference rooms in Port Moresby.'

Yes, but what story? Two other teachers I spoke to said Nobnob Primary is supposed to get 20,000 kina every quarter in school subsidies. But it's not news anymore that the money doesn't arrive on time or that, frequently, it doesn't arrive at all.

It's not shocking anymore that the kids don't get the support they need to achieve their dreams. It doesn't bother people that maybe the kid in the picture won't become a doctor because next year he'll have to stay home because dad's busy raising money to send his older brother to high school.

What story should I tell? This has become a repetition of stories with human faces. Faces we live with every day and ignore. But then, Nobnob may be fortunate to have teachers and classrooms and a road leading to Madang town. So what story should I tell?

Cleaners in Cairns Break Highlands Solidarity
By Joe Wasia

Sir Michael Somare's leadership has been brought to its knees and is in a questionable state after nine years of National Alliance Party rule.

PNG is an independent state, governed by its own constitution favouring democracy and the rights of its citizens. It is neither a family estate nor a family business where a family member has the right to inherit or pass on the leadership. This is despite the view amongst some people that PNG's prime ministership is personal business and can be passed down the line.

Sir Michael has promised that he will hand over the NA leadership and the PM prime ministership to someone in the party caucus before 2012. That said, deputy prime minister, highlander Don Polye, is the right candidate for both posts. Not Arthur Somare, as he is held by the throat by the National Court and that's a poor guarantee of his ability hold these posts in future.

The intention of Sir Michael and his cleaners from the highlands - namely Polye's own countrymen Peter Ipatas, Sam Abal, Anderson Angiru, and Peter O'Neil - shows how ill-minded and greedy people can become when they have a meeting in Cairns. All this served to do was to breach the solidity of the National Alliance in the highlands.

These self-serving leaders need to put away this mentality. After Paius Wingti was hailed as the first prime minister from the highlands region, there has been no other as many highlands cleaners supported the households of successive PMs from Momase, Islands and the Southern regions.

As far as we know, Polye is the right man for the job. He has maintained his integrity through political obstacles and has proven himself a true leader in tough times. Papua New Guineans have seen this. He is a man of integrity and dignity, unlike the creeds who crawled into Sir Mike's house to oppose Polye's appointment as PNG's prime minister.

This is ridiculous and utter nonsense. These people should blow away this mentality and work in union for a better highlands and PNG.

The Inevitable Growth of Global Sinophobia
By Bernard Yegiora

Anti-Chinese sentiment, or Sinophobia, is a deadly trend becoming more common as China continues to rise. It is defined as the dislike of or fear of China, its people or its culture.

Xenophobia, fear of foreigners, is widespread in all societies. In Iran, anti-American sentiment is strong. The Iranians see America as evil because of its arrogance. America, in its bid to create a peaceful world, has strongly gone against Iran's nuclear ambitions, even though Iran has assured the world that its nuclear program is for peaceful purposes.

In PNG's case, we witnessed the ransacking of Asian businesses in 2009; mostly targeting people of ethnic Chinese origin in major towns because of the disparity of wealth. This Sinophobia is growing and could lead to a major social uprising of greater magnitude in the future. Chinese entrepreneurs were in PNG a long time before independence and contributed immensely to PNG's development as a sovereign nation. This fact cannot be denied if you know your history.

Over more recent years, a new wave of Chinese immigrants and business activities have moved in a different pattern. The Chinese have adapted to the changes in PNG society, backed by their popular 'Guanxi system' that is similar to our 'wantok system'. We, on the other hand, have failed to evolve the way we do business. As a result, the lack of opportunity experienced by middle and low class citizens of this nation have led them to take out their frustrations on foreign owned businesses.

The reasons for this fear, or dislike, of the Chinese diasporas are very complex. It is like a triangle with three points of influence: government, citizens and Chinese entrepreneurs. It is difficult to accuse one factor as the root of the problem because all three have, in one way or another, played a significant part in feeding the growing anti-Chinese sentiment. PNG is just a needle in the haystack in the world of Sinophobia.

At state-to-state level, China's relationship with the different states in the international system reveals a sense of Sinophobia. Developed countries in Europe and Asia, including the world's declining hegemony America, from a realist perspective are fearful of China's rise because of the theory of balance of power.

After the Cold War, the bipolar world of the USSR and the US was disassembled and replaced with a uni-polar system controlled by the USA. But that order is changing, due to the remarkable rise of China affecting the balance of power as countries begin to join the Chinese bandwagon. The fear of China challenging America for the leadership position has led America to initiate containment and engagement plans to monitor China.

Furthermore, according to Robert Reich in New Perspective Quarterly, "China wants to become the world's pre-eminent producer nation". Reich draws a comparison between the US economy being oriented to consumption and the Chinese economy to production. This adds fuel to the fire because, with high production, China will continue to flood the world with 'Made in China' products affecting the balance of trade.

In a recent BBC/Globescan poll of 28 nations, China's global image remains mixed. Only in Africa and Pakistan is it consistently positive, while in Asia, North America and Latin America it is neutral to poor. Across Europe it is strongly negative. China's increasing economic and military power is creating anxiety around the world.

Thus, in this century, not only are Chinese traders victims of Sinophobia, but the Chinese State is enduring its share of anti-Chinese sentiment. This trend is unavoidable and will continue to intensify as China continues towards developed nation status.

THE AUTHORS

Kela Kapkora Sil Bolkin (38) was born in the Galkope area in the Simbu Province. He studied to become a Catholic priest but quit soon after completing his philosophical studies and attended the UPNG where he completed a BA majoring in Social Development and Anthropology. He also has a certificate of Leadership in Strategic Health Communication from the Johns Hopkins University (USA). He is now the Senior Policy Analyst at the National AIDS Council Secretariat in Port Moresby.

Bapa Bomoteng

Hinelou Nini Costigan (30) was born in Wewak in the East Sepik Province of mixed Australian and Manus parentage and grew up in Lae. She currently works overseas but comes home as often as possible. She comes from a large family which has produced a number of successful women and she aspires to emulate them.

Effrey Dademo (35) was born in Oro Province and grew up in the East New Britain Province. She has written poetry as a pastime since her student days at Kokopo Secondary School. She graduated from the University of Papua New Guinea in 1997 and was admitted to the Bar in 1998. She is the founder of Papua New Guinea's anti-corruption website *ACT NOW*. She has not actively pursued writing since her second year at law school due to study and work commitments but hopes to return to this pastime soon. She says she just needs some motivation.

Jimmy Drekore (38) comes from Sinasina in the Simbu Province, which he still calls home. He is an analytical chemist working on Lihir. When he is on leave he does charity work with the Simbu Children Foundation. He styles himself as a "bush poet" who "paints" poems in his quiet moments.

Jeffrey Febi (34) comes from Simbu Province. He is a geologist working in the oil and gas industry and lives with his wife and child in Port Moresby.

Writing and reading are his favourite hobbies and he has had some success in publishing his work locally.

Sharlene Kylie Gawi (27) was born in Lae with both Morobe and East Sepik connections. She enjoys reading, writing, singing and arts in general. She is a committed Christian who also believes in human rights.

Francis Hualupmoni (28) comes from East Sepik Province. He is currently living and studying in China for an MA in International Security. He is a graduate of UPNG with an honours degree in Political Science, specialising in International Relations. He works for the Office of Higher Education Research Science and Technology in Port Moresby He is also a freelance political researcher, analyst and writer.

"Icarus" was born in Port Moresby. He graduated from the University of Papua New Guinea and now works for a government organisation. He says he writes poetry because he likes to have his say. He also feels that poetry is often underestimated as a powerful means of expression for the collective conscience of people.

Janice Isu (31) comes from Hoskins on West New Britain. She loves to read and started writing both stories and poetry at high school. She is a lawyer by profession, lives in Port Moresby and is married with two young children.

Bette Carinya Kare (17) was born in Darwin. She is a student and lives with her widowed mother and sister. She writes to expand her imagination and to explore different issues and interests. She is a Peer Educator at the YWCA Adolescent Reproductive Health Program, a member of the Self Defence class and enjoys church and gospel music. She scored high disctinctions in all her year 10 subjects last year and has set her sights on becoming an Airforce Pilot.

Carolus Ketsimur (66) comes from Bougainville. He was a journalist for many years, working for both the ABC and the NBC, where he was their first program director. He returned to Bougainville in 1980 and is currently

Minister for Works, Transport and Communications in the government there. He is in the process of finalising a novel about black birding.

Mathias Kin (45) was born at Deri village in Salt Nomane Karimui District in the Simbu Province. He graduated from PNG Unitech in 1992 with a Bachelor of Science degree in Metallurgy. He works as an advisor with the Resettlement Project on the LNG Project; prior to that he was a public servant in Simbu for 14 years. He is married with 8 children.

David Kitchnoge (33) was born in Kainantu in the Eastern Highlands Province. His parents come from the East Sepik and Morobe Provinces. He is a graduate of the Divine Word University in Madang and is a financial manager living in Port Moresby. He regards himself as a rural product and is very passionate about rural development issues.

Eva Kuson (23) was born in the beautiful province of Manus but grew up in Port Moresby. She began writing and collecting short stories in 2009 as part of her feature writing class at Divine Word University. She hopes to soon publish a collection of stories from young writers around PNG's maritime provinces. She graduated from Divine Word University in 2011 with a Bachelor's Degree in Communication Arts (Journalism) and hopes to become a successful short story writer and journalist.

Lapieh Landu (22) was born in Port Moresby of mixed Eastern Highlands, Milne Bay and Sanduan parentage. She is a student at the Divine Word University in Madang studying international relations. She has been writing poetry since year 8 on a wide range of topics.

Mizraiim Lapa (27) comes from Ialibu in the Southern Highlands Province and works as a tax accountant in Port Moresby. She has been writing for over 10 years and finds it a relaxing and fulfilling activity.

Pochon S Lili (23) was born in Nauru but grew up in Port Moresby. His roots are in Manus Province. He has a degree in Business and Management and works for a large company in Port Moresby. He is passionate about human rights and uses writing as a way of expressing his views and opinions.

Francis Nii (48) was born at Yobai, Karimui Nomane in the Simbu Province. He has a degree in economics from UPNG and was a banker with the National Development Bank until an accident left him paraplegic. He is now a patient of the Kundiawa General Hospital. He has had an interest in writing since his UPNG days.

Martyn Namorong (25) was born at Baimuru in the Gulf Province and grew up in a logging camp at Kamusi on the border between Western and Gulf Provinces. His parents come from Madang and Western Province. He was a medical student at UPNG until 2009 but is now a street vendor and blogger.

Gelab Piak (23) was born in Port Moresby and is a student at the Divine Word University in Madang. He began writing poems in 2006. He also writes songs and short stories. He has a collection of poems ready for publication and is seeking a publisher.

Ignatius Piakal (33) comes from Enga Province but grew up in the shadow of Mount Mul in the Western Highlands Province. He is an environmentalist working for a non-government organisation teaching conservation in rural areas. He is also an advocate for literacy and dabbles in graphic and web design.

Patricia Paraide is from East New Britain. She has a Bed from UPNG, a Master's in Education Studies from Monash University and a PhD from Deakin University. She is now a senior research fellow at the National Institute and her work focuses on education issues in PNG. Patricia's husband, Daniel Patem, who died in December 2006, was Director General of National Libraries and Archives.

Fiona Yawewan Potane (19) comes from Wabag in Enga Province, which she still calls home. She is a student majoring in accounting with a minor in Spanish and loves soccer and kaukau. She is a passionate writer who regrets that there are no avenues in PNG to pursue it as a career.

Reginald Renagi (50+) comes from Central Province and lives in Port Moresby. He is a former naval officer and is now a professional trainer of sailors at PNG's new sea training school: Pacific Maritime Training College. His hobbies include reading and writing on a wide range of subjects; he is a regular contributor to newspapers and PNG Attitude. He hopes to write a book or two, including short stories and poems, for publication in the future.

Leonard Fong Roka (32) was born in Arawa and grew up in the Panguna District during the years of the Bougainville crisis. He began writing poetry as a student at Arawa High School and has now compiled a collection of short stories and poetry which he hopes to publish. He has returned after a break as a student at Divine Word University and is working on an autobiography of his experiences in the Bougainville war in his spare time.

Gina Samar (32) was born in Wewak in East Sepik Province and raised in Port Moresby, where she now works as an accountant. She began writing stories when she was 10 years old and thinks that had it been possible to make a living out of writing she might have pursued it as a career. She thinks that it is a pity that Port Moresby and PNG in general does not have many good bookstores and so few libraries.

Bernard Sinai (29) comes from Manus Province and now lives in Port Moresby. He started writing fiction while at college and published his first short story in 2006. Most of his work is fiction which draws heavily on his own real life experiences and those around him.

Scott Waide (34) was born in Goroka and spent much of his childhood in rural outstations of the Eastern Highlands and Morobe where his parents worked. He studied Journalism at Divine Word University and worked as a senior journalist and news anchor at EMTV for eight years before moving to work at the Australian Broadcasting Corporation's Port Moresby Bureau. Scott currently produces documentaries, web videos and articles aimed at highlighting developmental challenges faced by Papua New Guinean landowners.

Joe Wasia (22) is from the Wapenamanda district of the Enga Province and is in his final year of Environmental Health Sciences at Divine Word University in Madang, majoring in Occupational Health & Safety, He began writing for *PNG Attitude* about four years ago. He is interested in politics, business, reading novels, music (R&B, pop, hip hop) and telling stories. He is the 2011 President of the University's Enga Students Association.

Paul Waugla Drekore Wii

Imelda Yabara (35) was born in Port Moresby and lives in Madang. Her partner is a magistrate and she follows him around the country. She is the mother of two girls and, when time permits, loves writing. She has a blog at www.achingforpng@wordpress.com where she publishes her work.

Bernard Yegiora (27) was born in Kundiawa but his heritage is in Kubalia, East Sepik Province. His grandfather was one of the early colonial policemen from the coast who helped the Administration build the highway to the highlands. Here he found his wife to be in the Sinasina village of Koge, Simbu Province. Bernard started writing for the *Sunday Chronicle* in Mathew Yakai's *Letters from China* column in 2009 when he left for China to study. He hopes to one day publish a book about politics in PNG.

Tanya Zeriga-Alone (35) was born in Kainantu in the Eastern Highlands Province. Hergrandparents were missionaries with links to Morobe Province. She currently lives in Goroka and works as an environmental scientist for a non-government organisation as a planner/researcher. She is interested in photography, music, reading, politics and sewing.

www.ingramcontent.com/pod-product-compliance
Lightning Source LLC
Chambersburg PA
CBHW070920130626
46555CB00001B/215

* 9 7 8 0 9 8 7 1 3 2 1 0 9 *